Luck

A Force That Brings Good Fortune Or Adversity

Fortuna Alleno

ISBN : 1-4196-1473-8

To order additional copies, please contact us.
BookSurge, LLC
www.booksurge.com
1-866-308-6235
orders@booksurge.com

Luck

CHAPTERS

Dedicated To All Those Who Have Felt Unlucky At Some Time In Their Life.

I

Out of Luck

Switzerland

Karl is not lucky at the moment. He is sitting in cell 10 in a deeply conservative small town called St. Gallen, Switzerland. The townsmen of St. Gallen are very angry with him and his relative, who owns the local building company and who now finds himself bankrupt due to lending Karl 47 million Swiss francs from his company, which confirms that old cliché, never do business with family. The judges passed sentence on Karl and he will have to sit in prison for the next five years. All this is told to me over the car phone by my girlfriend that is married to him. Over the static, I put together that my old friend Karl is either one of the biggest frauds in Switzerland or he definitely needs something more than your routine heavy analysis. Karl, a Swiss financial advisor, has advised everyone around him, family, friends, lovers, wife, and local company to give him millions of francs to manage. Karl has managed to lose it all. Asked by the court when he thinks that he can pay it back, he answered "in fourteen days." The perfect answer from a seller of dreams. Now Karl sits in jail. Unanswered questions swarm around him. Did he put some money away for himself? Did he really think he could get away with it? Did he do it all for love of his wife? Does he really think that he is innocent as he claims he is? Or, is he a pure conman who has perfected his act through the years using my girlfriend as an accessory to complete the picture of successful advisor with that trusting smile? A mythomaniac or a simple Swiss boy whose head was turned with all the funds he was able to procure, starting in the good old times when the Arabs were rolling in money and he was a portfolio manager for one of the big three sister banks.

Tomorrow, my girlfriend will visit him in jail. Marie-Louise has, up until now, dreamed herself through life, but now that reality is knocking at her door she is seriously thinking of equipping herself for her next visit with a special recorder. She realizes she needs some hard evidence. Perhaps he will divulge some vital information to her during their meeting in jail. Marie-Louise has been trying to get divorced from Karl for years. But where is the money? Swiss men are masters of the universe at hiding their money away from everyone, including their nearest and dearest. It's in their genetic make-up. Making money, saving money, and hiding money. In terms of business, Swiss men are "usually in the money". They take their luck very seriously here. There is even an "Institut für Glücksforschung" (Institute for luck research).

2.

When You Realize You're not Lucky

Susan called me last night. She had had another vivid dream about her dead mother. "I kept asking my mother how she was, was she happy, free of pain," Susan recounted, "and my mother answered, stop thinking about clothes and shops. Go buy hotels." Umm, I muse, a mother giving business advice from the other side. How Swiss! I have a friend who only wants to go to heaven if she can ask her mother why she gave the house to her sister and not to her.

"Quite unusual," I answer.

"And then," Susan continues, "my mother insisted I speak to Peggy Roth. She said I knew her. That she was a journalist. I guess, I'll have to find her," Susan muttered, as she hung up the telephone. My mind raced through all the people I knew in the world hoping to find this name and save my friend from falling into a lifelong obsession in finding this person. It's as simple as that, you know. To fall into a quest that can take up your whole life.

People in the Swiss society often tell me about these kinds of experiences. In the practical hard working Swiss society that I graze around in, my kind of folk are thin pickings. Through the years, my curiosity has led me down quite a few exotic alternative paths and has tilted my sense of perception to include an even broader range of reality. Aah, reality, how we distort it and twist it to fit our own unique view. Is your present mate in the same reality as you? You know exactly what I mean, and if you don't, I am sorry. I cannot explain it right now, for I want to get onto the only important question I want to know the answer to. It shapes all our lives and nobody ever discusses it. My question is: What is luck and how can I get some of it?

I remember the moment when the realization hit me that I was not lucky. I was in my bedroom talking to someone on the telephone. As I hung up, the thought crossed through my mind like a blinding flash. I simply was not lucky. If I had been, by now I would have had the happy marriage, the successful business, and a life filled with wonderful friends, successful children, and so on. With me, everything was almost, but not quite there. I was lucky, of course, that I wasn't born into some wartorn country. But luck is always relative to one's own surroundings.

So, my question to myself was, Fortuna, what do you do when you realize you're not lucky, and how do you become luckier?

3·

Personal Thoughts on Luck

People that have very little luck can think they are lucky.
    People that have a lot of luck don't necessarily think they're lucky.
    I don't have it.
    Bad luck visits countries,

        Whole families,
        Groups of friends (watch who your friends are).

Good luck is more singular.

        Lottery winners.
        One happy family you know of.
        A boy or a girl who has beauty and brains and makes the most out of it.
        People who were trained to think they are special think they are lucky.
        People who believe themselves special by God's right consider themselves lucky.
        People who have gotten what they want and are smugly content.

 If you have luck, should you push your luck?

        The golden touch (luck).

People have cheated to get their luck.
Lucky Duck, Lucky Star, Lucky Charm.

May the luck of the Irish be with you (why the Irish?).
Lucky in cards, unlucky in love.
Lucky break.
You don't know if you have been truly lucky till the end of your life. One can have good luck at the beginning of one's life, but then it turns and the rest is unlucky. Or, your good luck is so wonderful towards the end of your life that it cancels out the earlier unlucky times.

4.

Wrong Timing

I love talking to Catherine. It is always so stimulating and we always come up with such wonderful ideas. To make money with, of course. They are always, I think, original and great money-spinners. Why haven't any of them come to anything?

Wrong timing, people say. Is it? Are we always too early or too late? What does that mean? How do you know when the time is right? Do you know? What does it mean "being at the right place at the right time"? Time is not merely the measure of our days. Time is a reality in its own right as much as a dimension. It is an element totally involved in the evolution of the human spirit. It has a character of its own that it communicates to life. It is intertwined with our spiritual evolution. Everything in life not only has its own reality, but also a time character that is shared with all other things existing at that unique moment. There is not one idea or action that is free of it; growth is possible only in so far as it corresponds in time to the overall character, "the great togetherness". All living things, consciously or unconsciously, partake of that character in any moment of time. It is shared no matter where they are.

It is perhaps correct what the American Indians say, there is no right time. When it is the right time, then you are there. I doubt that all our ideas are bad and we certainly have the energy to see them through. I have a sneaking suspicion it has to do with luck, don't you?—Or is it "synchronicity" where certain events in time happen together; ummm, more on that later.

But then again, I could pendle this question. Lately I have been pendling everything. Whenever a question comes up that I'm not sure about, whether it's a friend who is undecided or I don't know what stock to buy or what food is good for me, I pendle (also known as dowsing). Pendling, for you out there who do not walk the same paths as I do, is the practice of taking a pendulum (a small object made out of glass, wood, metal, or simply a wedding band will do), attaching a long string to it, and holding it over a written question and/or object. You then proceed to ask your question. If the pendulum swings in a clockwise circle, the answer is yes, anticlockwise, it's no. Don't laugh, it is deadly accurate and has been used throughout the centuries for divining water, metals, and life situations. As of today, there are many theories why it works. My own feeling about it is that we act like radio antennas and are able to pick up these energy patterns by concentrating our thoughts. This method can really save you years of romantic folly, bad choices in work, etc. It comes down to compatible energy fields. Unfortunately, the one question I am obsessed with, it has not answered. Why aren't I lucky? I have asked it late at night when perhaps the gods are asleep; I have couched the question in a thousand sneaky formations to no avail, and so have contented myself with the mundane questions of life which it answers very well. But when it comes to luck, it stops still and will not budge.

5.

Chance Meeting

Marie-Louise has come back from visiting Karl in prison. We are tossing around Karl's unluckiness and his ability to always find some good luck in his back luck. Karl's bankruptcy will be listed in the newspapers next week and that means the local officials will be at their house writing down everything she has so that it can be used to pay back his debts. Right now, I know of two other families doing this. One, a well-known banker who from pure greed was laundering money through his Geneva bank and, to his unluckiness, was caught; the other one being from bad business decisions. Maybe they should include this in the marriage contract in Switzerland. If due to excessive greed you, or your spouse, are caught with your hand in the till, the other must be able to react quickly to liquidate and dispense away all ready assets immediately. Women would be given a test to see how fast they could disperse their family fortune.

Marie-Louise tells me of all these new developments while we are on our way to Lausanne. We are seated across our lovely lunchtime table on this Swiss train from a man who catches both our interests. He is writing in longhand (actually using a pen) into a lovely bound notebook. We are mesmerized for one minute. All around us, men are talking into their new plaything, their mobile phones. Laptop computers are perched on business legs and snatches of business conversations are in the air. After all, this is the commuter lunchtime train from Zürich to Lausanne. Who is this man? Being women, we must know, especially since he has such a beautiful handwriting—large and generous with big swirls reaching to the end of the page.

Dr Jean Pito, a big burlish teddy bear of a man turns out to be the director of one of Switzerland's leading advertising agencies. He is a Basler living in Bern and is in the process of writing an introduction to an artists' catalogue. We immediately click and start to gossip about everyone in Switzerland. Switzerland is a very small country and if you live there long enough you just about know everyone's story, whether you know them or not. After going through the latest financial debacles that had been in the papers I get to my other problem—launching my Swiss conductors' handbag. I have adapted this most famous of conductors' bags for women. Can you imagine pulling into a grey, somber Zürich train station one morning and seeing these serious Swiss conductors wearing bright red bags, sensuously curved in design, worn over their shoulders with straps literally reaching down to their toes. Well, I loved that outrageous bag and eventually found the original producers hidden away in the Swiss countryside. Selling it privately has been a big success, but I want to make it a more commercial enterprise. Could he suggest what to do? His eyes dance with amazement. Only last week he showed this bag to one of his biggest clients as a symbol of Swiss workmanship and style. He was willing to meet with me again. A week later, we met and I showed him my bags and belts. All excited with my line, he agreed to show it to his clients. His parting words were, "We just need a little luck."

6.

Luck, French Style

The French, a folk who have built their culture upon the Cartesian model of reason and logic, go to more fortune-tellers than any other nation in Europe. They have divided luck in their logical manner into three categories:

1. **La fortune**
   It just happens. You win the lottery. This is the purest form of luck. It has nothing to do with your emotions.

2. **La chance**
   Here you make your luck through your effort.

3. **Le bonheur**
   The happiness within you is luck.

7.

Karma in Luck

Club Med

Club Med was started by the French to make the normally anti-social French talk to each other at least on holiday. It is a world-wide organization with clubs scattered all over the world offering in winter or summer, sports, entertainment, good food, facilities for the whole family to enjoy a holiday, and the chance to fall in love for at least a week. At breakfast, lunch and dinner you are thrown together at large round tables where you desperately think of things to say to people you have nothing in common with. "An exercise in social interaction," I tell my normally shy son who is totally overwhelmed by it all. I mean, what does he say to the older Japanese man to his right and the beautiful young French girl to his left who he could lonely dream about meeting, but is now actually sitting next to, totally tongue-tied. The beautiful young employees of the Club flitter here and there, thin and gorgeous, creating an atmosphere of youth and fun. A relentless cheerfulness fills the air. To be depressed here is not possible.

We are in Tignes Val Claret for skiing, situated on top of France's glacier, the Grand Motte. The sun is shining, lots of fresh snow covers the mountains, and we are here to bring in the New Year of 1995. I have found myself in the company of three older English men, away from their wives for the week; we are having dinner together in the smaller restaurant that the Club offers if you want a more intimate atmosphere. They are older men, successful, satisfied with their lives, witty, charming, and urbane. Perfect for my question. The atmosphere is warm and lively, and in a moment of lull in the conversation I ask them. "Gentlemen, I would like your opinion. What do you think luck is?"

"That's easy," Derek quickly responds, "the world is chaos and sometimes somehow two forces of energy come together and sometimes it works."

"No, that's too easy what you say," says Simon, a well-known manager of rock stars in London. "One needs the preparation for luck. Getting your own house in order and when the opportunity comes along being wise enough to take it. Of course, there are different kinds of luck. You can be sitting on a ski lift and next to you is your soul-mate for life. That luck is different; it falls into clusters of souls from other lives, of course." Blank stares confront him. We are ready to fall off the world and unconsciously his two friends of thirty years pull him back.

"Rubbish," says Derek, "you can't really believe in other lives, Karma and all that. One's perception of reality is hard enough to deal with in this world, let alone past lives." As the discussion swirls around me I realize I should be putting this question to a philosopher, but I don't know any. I only seem to know names of politicians, movie stars, computer engineers, and scientists. Maybe Bill Gates knows what luck is. Maybe it's in one of his computer programs and all one has to do is download the answer from his database of information.

8.

Psychic luck

London

Mary has been a practicing transmedium for twenty-five years.
I have made an appointment with her today at the College
of Psychic Studies. I am quite excited. I don't know what to
expect; I hope it's not too spiritual, future fortune-telling
instead. I'll have to work on my lack of religious fervor the next
time around and hope there's a nice angel looking over me.

Mary sits at the far end of an almost bare room. Just a
chair for me and a table separates us. A tape recorder is there
for my use if I want to record the session. A nice middle-aged
English woman greets me. She explains to me that it will take
her a few minutes to get into her trance. I watch, mesmerized,
as the air around her wavers and an old Chinese man starts to
talk through her. In English, of course, but Mary's prim sitting
position has changed into an old man's sitting position, legs
open, Mary leans forward to me, her gestures are masculine and
demanding. I listen transfixed. What she tells me I have waited
my whole life to hear.

"You see, we are all part of the force of the Universe. The
Universe is a prism in expansion and that same force that which
expands the Universe is that force which animates you. You have
a personality, sexuality, character. But all that is not you. You are
the animation of the outer being. The you, that is the animation
which is the force. This force, because it is in expansion, is

pulsating and a pulsation makes a sound and a sound makes a color. And all this goes out from us. The color, the reaction to life, and I add or subtract color according to my reaction to my experiences. So that nothing happens to me that I am not actually putting out in a way. If I put this color out such a thing will eventually come back towards me." Mary continues, "for when you have your heart and head in balance that is when we are beginning to give off the force which produces something that will fulfill you. You must send out your colored ribbons to attract what you want. The rate of movement of the force creates the color. The stronger this force is the more it will attract that which will fulfill you. That is what I call luck."

It seems one must simply get one's colors in order. Mine were overflowing all over the place. I must tidy them up. I never thought luck had anything to do with throwing out the right ribbons.

As I continue to listen to her, my mind on another level is asking how is this transformation possible. It is really happening before my eyes. She is telling me amazing things about myself and the people I know. I think about a lecture given by Dr Marie-Louise von Franz, a co-worker of CG Jung's, and an acknowledged authority on the psychological interpretation of dreams, myths, alchemy, and fairy tales. She explained that she had gone to a famous Dutch palmist to have her palm read and was so amazed at what he said that she continued to delve into how he could have possibly come up with all this information. Her conclusion was that he was able to draw on what Jung called the "absolute knowledge of the unconscious", which she knew existed from her work with dreams. Jung told her the unconscious knows things. It knows the past and the future. It knows about other people. We have all had dreams that informed us about something which happened to someone we knew. Jung has said that the earliest dream of a child sometimes anticipates his whole life.

Look into a child's dream and see the seed of a life, which later will be a full-grown tree. Ask your two-year old what he/she dreamed about last night, it might save you thousands of dollars later in psychologists' fees or in useless years of studies in the wrong profession. Mediums, such as Mary or this Dutch palmist, have a closer relationship to the unconscious than the rest of us. They are just nearer to this absolute knowledge and their conscious mind is not as conditioned as ours is to block out the unconscious. They need only to scramble their minds and let the unconscious surface. We seem only to let our unconscious come through in our daydreams, or night dreams, or by the famous slips of the tongue.

But Mary and all the diviners before her have reached the unconscious by another way. The French psychologist, Pierre Janet used the term "abaissement du niveau mental," to lower a mental threshold and go into a trance, a sleep-like state, to pull up this knowledge. This has been done either by looking at chaotic patterns such as tea leaves, water, cards, and crystal balls, or even dancing to near exhaustion. All ways to scramble and lower that sharp conscious mind of ours.

Jung believed at such times the unconscious is heightened and comes under the influence of the archetypes belonging to the collective unconscious. In responding to the force of psychological patterns, human beings can find themselves in various altering relationships with the external world. This manifestation can be the famous coincidences that we all have: thinking about someone, then shortly after bumping into them, people calling each other on the telephone at the same time. Jung was convinced that there was some linking process at work in the Universe, collaboration between the human psyche and the external world that transcended established laws of physics. He named this principle synchronicity and devoted much of his later years to explaining it. More on this later. Right now, I am not letting Mary off the hook, I continue.

"I am writing this book, believe it or not, on luck."

Mary: "Oh, I'm a great believer in luck."

(I am surprised at her enthusiasm): "Oh, are you?"

Mary: "It's actually working with the force of your own energy and once you get into the force of your energy—oh how lucky!—You've reached a deeper part of self where there is what you call luck because there is infinite knowledge. So having infinite knowledge certainly gives one luck. So accept that it's there. Luck we see as random, but I see luck as the digestion of my own knowledge."

(I'm not letting her off): "Yes, but I'll ask you something else. Some horrible criminal, he wins the lottery. Now people would say that's luck. He's not done anything good. He's not worked on himself. How would you explain it?"

Mary: "But we don't know what his Karma is."

(It's the ole Karma story, I think): "Well, I see you are bringing in something very different now."

Mary: "Oh, now we are saying because he has many bags of gold that he's lucky. This doesn't necessary mean he's lucky. He can say, 'and they all want money from me' and 'that girl doesn't like me even with all this money'. Is this really luck? It seems like it is only because in our viewing we measure the quality of ourselves by the amount of bags of gold we have. That's got nothing to do with it. The bags of gold will not satisfy the emotional hunger, they will not necessarily bring you health, they will not bring you the joy of creativity."

"Thank you again."

Mary: "If one day you win the lottery, look well at what you've got. See what that really means for you. Certainly do it for yourself. Oh, I have always wanted this or that ... Do it and see what it really means. I've done it now. Don't act quickly in moments of what seems like excellent fortune. Keep your balance. I will go now ..."

Having lots of money does not

necessarily bring you luck

9.

London 1995

What do the top men of one of London's leading auction houses talk about when they are gathered together to discuss the strategy of acquiring an art collection consisting of over 10,000 paintings that I have brought to them. Yes, there are large collections like this. The handsome English Collector showed me this overwhelming collection neatly stacked away at the Port Franc in Geneva. Now that's a lot of work I thought as I asked for a glass of water before I began the job of assessing if I could make a market for them. I had naively thought as we walked over to the storage area that I would be looking at 25, maybe 50 paintings. But there is always a bigger collection for sale and, in my search to find a buyer, a representative of a Middle Eastern country informed me that, actually, my collection was quite small. He said he had just bought the entire collection of a middle European country, which had been sold to the state in exchange for grain. I didn't believe him, you wouldn't have either if you knew the amount, or, how could they own the entire cultural heritage of a country. The dealer was called up and confirmed the sale. Our collection was not so big after all, and the paintings were OK, secondary market, early 20th Century, decorative, I knew I could place them, but unfortunately not with him.

So, here I am seated with the men who make this famous auction house move. Seven men and myself. Are they going to talk about the aesthetic values of the art collection, the historical value, the commercial value? Well yes, these were touched upon, but what they really wanted to discuss was how old everyone thought the collector was, sixty/seventy or a very well preserved eighty? I've had this before when I found myself immersed in a conversation with the top-level men representing one of South America's leading politicians talking about if he had a face-lift or a tummytuck. I thought women only went in for this type of talk. Well, it shows that the Roman standards of beauty have taken over at every level. I can just imagine scientists gathering at a conference for new studies on the superstring theory and instead are huddling in corners discussing if the leading practitioner, Edward Witten didn't look well, rather younger looking, something around the eyes, not quite sure of what it could be — eye surgery? Interesting about science, today's science. They have established beyond reasonable doubt the existence of atoms, elements, DNA, bacteria, stars and galaxies, gravity and electromagnetism, but they have left many mysteries unsolved. Like, is there life on other planets? How does our mind work? Behind the questions lurks the other bigger question. Why is there something rather than nothing and since there is something, is there a plan to the whole thing, and where does chance fit in? God, the human being really does like making up unanswerable questions, then making up fabulous theories no one can prove. Well, it keeps a lot of us busy fantasizing. Were we humans just a fluke of nature? I would like to see a meeting with these top scientists, a few philosophers, some religious leaders, a sprinkling of indigenous people still carrying the original myths in stones with them, and see what they come up with. They probably wind up in the corner discussing the best retreats for rejuvenation. So, it looks like I cannot turn to the scientific community for help with my search on luck. If it can't be measured in a clinical trial they are just not interested. Also, how can you patent luck? There are a few pioneers such as Dr. Daniel Bohm, a professor of Theoretical Physics at London's Birbeck College. In Bohm`s worldview, he tries to give a coherent understanding of physical phenomenon and has touched upon the area we are concerned about. He suggests that both the material world and consciousness are parts of a single unbroken totality of movement. His wedding of physics and consciousness has certainly woken up the scientific community, particularly coming from someone who is not airyfairy or a new-age mumbo-jumbo person. He suggests there is a level of reality beyond our normal everyday thoughts and perceptions. This, he calls, the explicit order. Then there is an implicit order, where the totality of existence is enfolded within each fragment of space and time—whether it is a single object, thought or an event. Thus everything in the Universe affects everything else because they are all part of the same unbroken whole. JS Bell, a Swiss physicist, backed up Bohm's worldview. He proposed in 1964 the theorem of the oneness of the sub-atomic world. It was experimentally confirmed eight years later by the physicist Alain Aspect at the University of Paris and means that the world is fundamentally inseparable. We are all one. As Mary the psychic had told me. The scientific community has come to the same conclusion via the particles. As Dr Bohm's theory elaborates, this comes back to all knowledge is in us. We are actually the whole of mankind. The entire past is enfolded in each one of us. Everything is enfolded in everything and also, I am sure, is our present and future. Our luck lies in knowing ourselves. Then, you are open and can tap the Universe.

I can only end this Chapter by saying that many scientists are superstitious and when two Chinese-American scientists, Chen Ning Yang and Tsung-Dao Lee, had to decide whether to continue their experiments in Particle Physics, they consulted their copy of the I Ching, the ancient Chinese book of prophecy. The answer told them to persevere with conviction and the two went on to win the Nobel Prize in 1959. Niels Bohr, Nobel Prize winning scientist, when asked why he had a rabbit's foot pinned to his laboratory door, said, "I'm told it brings luck whether one believes in it or not."

10.

Impatient with Luck

California

I am staying with my brother in not so sunny California. It's May, the weather should be splendid, but weather patterns in America are acting up and I've had to do with cool, rainy weather so far. Two weeks ago, my brother called me up and told me he was losing it. His manic-depressive ex-cheerleader wife had finally brought to the surface all that underlying aggression she was containing for years and now had let it out. In their dance of divorce, my six-foot-two, 250-pound brother realizes he's no match for a woman who realizes her meal ticket is leaving and she will have to confront herself and take control of her life. Child women are not into self-examination and working on themselves. Denial has worked for her, her whole life, and she doesn't want to try something new.

Well, I'm here helping him organize the transition and, since he's asked for full custody, the realization has hit him that being a single parent needs some organization. I think he'll do a great job once it's settled down. He's financially better off so he can give Jay a better education, can help him with all the sciences coming up, and he's crazy about the kid. Sorry feminists, rearing children goes to the best one qualified to do it in my book. Jay, their eight-year old son is your typical snub-nosed, blue-eyed, Sega game obsessed child, is already bored with the two of them fighting and pushed the situation along

last night by demanding new step-parents. He had my brother
write down what he wanted in his new step-mom:

1.   She mustn't yell at me, just talk to me.
2.   Be kind.
3.   She has to have a job and have money, and
4.   She should have a different name than his mom.

There's an eight-year old boy that's light years ahead of his
parents.

By the way, I don't like California, not for the obvious
reasons, mindless, formless, sprawling new communities and
shopping centers, crime, smog etc. The reason is that if you
stand in front of an enormous ocean and you don't smell the
sea air, what's the point of it all. Even the cut grass here doesn't
smell, plus all the food is tasteless. It's like eating cardboard
with lots of sauces on it. The tasteless tomatoes look wonderful,
no smell of course, huge tasteless chickens look grand but zero
taste. Maybe that's why the Californians compensate visually.
All those glistening capped teeth flashing at me. All those nose
jobs, lip jobs, breast jobs. Well, I could go on, but what is still
nice about California is that people still believe in the American
dream and still want to make it. They still want to become that
famous actress or actor. I had lunch with a not so young actress
yesterday. Full of ambition, she brimmed over with excitement.
Margaret had already signed two contracts for two major
pictures coming up and her parts were good. It seemed her luck
had changed. Other roles were piled up for her to play and one
could see her sweet husband, a housepainter, was already lost to
her and her ambitions. "It's about time my luck has changed,"
she yelled out over the crowded restaurant we were all sitting
in. Impatient with luck. Which brings me back to the purpose
of this story. That's how my nephew feels right now. Last night,
Jay came home with my brother like a little bull in a china shop,
all motion and aggression. He was getting impatient. He hadn't
won anything at McDonald's.

"Dad, will we win something?"

" Maybe, Jay, if you're lucky."

"What's lucky?"

"Well, someone out there will win some of those McDonald's prizes. If you are one of those people you are lucky. For the chances of winning are very small." "Your see," my brother elaborates, "I am a pessimist, I don't think I'll win anything. If I do win I'll be happily surprised. Up till now, I've never won a prize. Or, you can be an optimist, like your aunt and think you're going to win all the time. She enjoys thinking she's going to win and when she loses she's disappointed. But being an optimist doesn't automatically mean you're going to win either. So, Jay, are you an optimist or a pessimist?"

"I don't know Dad. It's a hard question; I'd just rather be lucky instead."

II

Reality versus Luck

"I have no money," whines Marie-Louise. "I keep paying these enormous bills while Karl sits in prison. Happy! He says he is happy! In a few years he will come out with no debts; in the meantime I must pay and pay. What should I do? My banker told me that from the settlement I'll probably receive from Karl it will just about cover my monthly telephone bill. I can't live on that!" By now, you realize that Marie-Louise has never thought about the alternative that most people turn to when they have no money. They work. It is a beautiful night on the Zürich Sea, and as I look around at the contented Swiss Burghers eating their Egli filets it is hard to imagine that people in Switzerland can go bankrupt, have all their possessions taken away from them, and go to prison.

I gently bring up the subject of work. "Well you know Marie-Louise, if you want to know how most people do it, they work."

"Work! What kind of money can you make working. Kill yourself for 5000 francs a month and then you have nothing at the end of the month. No, that's no good."

"But, Marie-Louise, if you keep spending your capital like you are doing and nothing is coming in you simply will have no money left" (basics 101 in money management—very few women have taken this course). This doesn't seem a solution to her problem and so what is left is the only solution that women of all ages have always turned to. She must find a new husband, immediately. Anyone will do, well not anyone. One wonders who is living more in a dream world. Her fantasist ex-husband, living in prison, liking his job as the head gardener and developing a new flower to be named after himself, probably 'Conmanius', a flower that smells sweet, but if you touch it sucks out any valuables you have on you. Or his ex-wife who never thought she would have to worry about money and continues to spend and watch her account dwindle. Marie-Louise says she will try to be more realistic. She just wants a 'normal guy', someone very wealthy, good looking, around fifty, and who knows how to enjoy life. Lots of luck!

12.

Lucky in Love

Yes, there are still fairy tale love stories. My Brazilian hairdresser has met the man of her life. A handsome rich banker who has fallen madly in love with her and has asked her to marry him. Their eyes met across a crowded restaurant and somehow they knew this was it. All this is told to me in a Zürich coffee shop. The wedding will be held at a famous Hotel in the Palais Schwarzenberg in Vienna. People will be flying in from around the world. I glory in her happiness and then she turns to me and tells me that they have decided they want me to be the matron of honor at their wedding. I am totally touched. No one in my whole life has made such a gesture to me. Tears come to my eyes. I accept and am delighted to join in the fun. She explains to me that all her girlfriends will be so jealous. Why should she have all the luck, luck, luck.

Three months later, I find myself on a sweltering June day landing in the land of Mozart and apple strudel. Vienna is an impressive city; one is aware of the glorious past of the Austrian Empire. The magnificent buildings have been spruced up and some modern Austrian architecture tastefully added. New Champagne bars are interspersed in between beer stubens and the tradition of gathering in coffeehouses is still ever present. From the looks of the local folks after a lifetime of beer drinking, wine drinking, apple strudel eating, and Champagne sipping, most of them have the choice of an early heart attack or definitely be a candidate for the local Alcohol Anonymous.

But I am not here to worry about the health habits of the Viennese. I'm here for the wedding and so at 5.00 pm on a warm summer night I am driven up to the beautiful entrance of the Palais Schwarzenberg. First commissioned by Prince Heinrich von Mansfeld-Fondi and then taken over by Prince Adam Franz zu Schwarzenberg, the palace was completed in 1732. It now sits quite comfortably in the center of Vienna nestled in front of its own gardens. Part of the Palais has been turned into a hotel and the wedding will be held in the five stately baroque rooms available for today's fest. I enter a spectacular entrance hall and walk towards the guests that are assembled. Don't ever worry what to wear to a wedding in Europe. It's black and more black. How drab everyone looked. How did we all become so timid with out clothes? I guess I can blame it on Coco Chanel who said the little black dress was the chicest thing you could ever wear. What a shame! I think we should go back to designing our own clothes anyway. All the clothes designed now are for young girls who have perfect bodies and women over a certain age have no clothes to choose from. I close my eyes and imagine how wonderful the clothes would have been to match the decor in the 1730s. Women don't give up, look beautiful for your men. And don't all you people give in totally to the computer world and its email. Recently, I was in Florence and I bought some really beautiful stationery. It is made out of linen using the same process they've used since the 14th Century. Those Italians wanted their love letters to last. It's wonderful to receive a letter from someone. And a lover's letter is the best. First, the slight shock of recognizing your lover's handwriting, then being afraid to open it, the talking to it, the reading of it in your hands, over and over. It's wonderful. The English still write letters for every occasion. Keep it up.

One should never ask a philosophical question until the end of a meal and now I turn to a young Austrian man seated next to me and ask him what he thinks luck is. He is a young banker and seems to show a certain sensitivity and wisdom beyond his thirty something years. The young couples sprinkled around the table are friendly and curious to hear his answer. "It is all wrapped up with being happy within yourself, isn't it. One must turn whatever one experiences into a positive experience. The hardest of all is to know what you really want and that comes from deep inside yourself. What you really want must not be based on superficial exterior goals, money, homes, and success for the ego. I think the luck is when deep down inside your soul you know what you want and you live that." Not bad.

Harold, the bridegroom gives a beautiful speech on the lawn after the dinner saying that he knew what he wanted in a woman. He wanted a woman who was lively, warm hearted, flexible, and exotic, and when he met Maria his heart knew. He had found the woman of his dreams. He was the luckiest person in the world!

Hans in Luck

Fairy tale Luck

(Hans im Glück, German fairy tale)

There is an old fairy tale that all Swiss children know. It is the story of a little boy who, after working seven long years for his master, is paid for his work with a big piece of gold (naturally, what else would he get in Switzerland). He starts his trip home, but on the way he finds his piece of gold is too heavy to carry. As luck would have it, he meets a man who is willing to exchange his horse for Hans' piece of gold. Now Hans is happy; he does not have to carry his heavy piece of gold and can ride his horse in comfort. But what good is a horse if you are thirsty and Hans finds that he is getting very thirsty. Now Hans is lucky again, for he meets someone who is willing to take his horse and give him his cow. But Hans quickly finds out that the cow is too old and no milk is possible. He then meets a man who is willing to take the cow and give him a pig instead. Umm, Hans thinks, good meat I can have with this animal, so he takes the pig. As he continues his voyage, he meets another man who tells him that he has a stolen goose and if he is caught he will be in a lot of trouble. Hans changes his pig for a goose and thinks again how lucky he is to have feathers for his pillow, goosefat for the winter, and the goose to eat. How well he will sleep. As he comes to the last village before he reaches his home, he sees a man grinding scissors. While the man is sharpening the knives, he tells Hans what a wonderful job he has; all he needs is his whetstone to sharpen the cutlery and he can make money from this. Oh how lucky, says Hans, all I need is this stone and I will be the happiest boy. He throws the man the goose and takes the heavy stone on his shoulder. I must really have been born in a lucky skin as everything that I want comes to me. Hans continues his journey. Eventually he becomes thirsty and puts down the stone on the side of the bridge while he drinks some water. Naturally, the stone falls into the water and Hans is left with nothing. Hans, with tears in his eyes, thanks God for taking this heavy burden away that he was carrying.He yells "I am so lucky, I am the luckiest person in the world and with a light heart and totally free he runs home to his mother."

Lessons to be learned:

1. Hans was the most stupid child you ever met.
2. He saw the bright side of every situation that confronted him, therefore he was a happy person.
3. He believed he was lucky, therefore he was lucky.
4. There was one mad mother when he got home, but that's beside the point.
5. Or, the moral of the story is (there is always one) that a man who has no material possessions to worry about is truly free, for with every possession there is a worry and fear which leaves less room for luck or happiness. Hans was truly a lucky and happy person.
6. Now, if it was my family, they would be out looking for that horse trader with the gold, pushing our luck in the hope we could find him. Fairy tale ended.

Luck is treated as one of our

superficial states of being. Tossed around

lightly 'lots of luck! '

But the truth is, we all take luck

deadly serious!!!

(Fortuna Alleno)

14.

Lucky People

'Some people have a bigger piece of luck than others'
True

There are people born under a lucky star. They know it. Their whole life basically falls into place for them. They don't work on being lucky, they just are. They have the genetic gifts of good health and intelligence and they represent the specific goals of their culture. In our Western culture, that would be slim, rich, educated, well liked, sportive, and successful in business, maybe an actress or model for a woman. These people are able to replicate the ideal physical and social image of our historical time and place. They are considered lucky people. At the other end exists the truly unlucky person, utterly unlucky in most every aspect of their lives. Well, for these people, 'better luck next time'. But if you fall in the middle like most people, you can increase your chances of luck by encouraging a more positive outlook in what you're trying to attain. A noted authority on superstition gives us his advice. "If a man or woman performs some little act because they think it will bring them luck then the chances are that it will do so because the layers of self-doubt which inhibit so many of our actions have been seeded with positive thought. Superstitions and the rituals attending them work because it is belief operating at its most potent level, that is of the subconscious, one could call it positive conditioning. So, Good Luck can be beckoned. There is a psychological connection and it comes to rich and poor."

*'I believe in luck. How else can you explain the success of those you
dislike.'*
Jean Cocteau

15.

Lucky Charms etc.

'Depend on the rabbit's foot if you will, but remember it didn't work for the rabbit.'
R E Shay

Throughout history, oracles, wise men, and ordinary people have tried to second-guess what the future holds for them. They would try clairvoyance, Psychics, Gurus, Astrology, Dreams, Runes, Palmistry, Numerology, tea leaves, Tarot cards, and crystal balls. But it was usually a hit or miss affair. What wise men did observe through the centuries was that there were definitely certain days, numbers and objects that were just luckier than others were. Most of them still survive to this day, proving their staying power. Look in any student's pocket on his test day and you'll probably find one of these ancient amulets of good luck.

What follows is a list of those tried and true centuries old lucky pieces:

- Carry around an amulet. These are religious objects or inscriptions from religious crosses, a Buddha, Mezuzahs, Catholic Saints, Chinese jade. They ward off bad energy and court good fortune.
- Own some lucky coins (Chinese or American).
- Women should own a Charm bracelet; a heart and key should be on it. Key rings should carry a lucky number or lucky animal: elephants, scarab beetles, pigs, or a small teddy bear. Don't forget a rabbit's foot.

- Have some jewelry made out of Jade, Lapis Lazuli or your own birthstone. They are considered lucky.
- Eat some lucky food: the Amanita muscaria mushroom and the Frijol Colorado are considered lucky.
- For a fertility charm: carry around a frog made out of jade (Chinese) or a frog made out of Amber (old Roman), a penis amulet (Asia), Raccoon penis bones (America), a Saint Anthony charm.
- Know some magic words: Abracadabra will do.
- Put some Holly up at Christmas time.
- Have in your possession a Talisman (Talismans are objects charged with extraordinary positive powers which can be duly transferred to the possessor); magic wands, Aladdin's magic lamp and King Arthur's magic sword, the Excalibur, are examples. They are imbued with protective powers by nature, by the gods, by magic or by the concentrated mind of the willful holder. The important thing is that the owner believes it has the power to protect against misfortune.
- And if you see a falling star, a seven-holed horseshoe, a Lady Bug, a Bluebird, a four-leaf clover, a Chimney Sweep (but you must shake hands with him), or a rainbow—it will bring you luck.
- Watch for Jupiter, planet of luck and good fortune, when it comes into the right place in your astrological chart.

16.

Lucky Numbers

*'This is the third time; I hope good luck lies in odd numbers ...
There is divinity in odd numbers, either in nativity, chance or
death.'*
(Source: Merry Wives of Windsor, v. 1.2, William Shakespeare)

Numbers Are Powerful
- If we do not understand somebody, we say we have not got his number, meaning we have not the frequency or the radar beam to get in touch with that personality.
- We identify with individual numbers, especially the Chinese.
- We believe we can handle an infinite series of natural numbers, in reality we are only handling abstract concepts.
- Sayings: "I've got your number," " What a cute number", "I number him among my friends", "She's number one in my book," "What's your lucky number?" "His number is up."

Pick a Lucky Number: Three
Three is a very lucky number. Pythagoras deemed it 'the perfect number', a symbol of completion and fertility. It is man and woman coming together and making the third.

The Holy Trinity

Past, Future, Present

Information, Energy, Matter (Modern Science)

The Three Fates
Body, Mind, Soul
Three Cheers
Three Chances
Codon, Psychon, Somaton (Biology DNA)
Fortune, good and bad, runs in three:

> Third time lucky,
> Three on a match,
> Three times and you're out

The Number Seven

Seven is a very powerful number and has its origin in the early beginnings of a civilization:

> Seven seas
> Seven notes on the scale
> Seven wonders of the Ancient World
> Seven ages of man
> The notorious Seven Year itch
> God rested on the Seventh Day
> A lucky number at the craps table

Seven is the number that occurs most often according to the laws of probability.

17.

Fortuna Lady Luck

A Rabbi said
'Life, sons and wealth do not depend upon merit, but upon luck'

I walk almost every day to start my muse working. Sometimes it works, sometimes not. Walking around Hyde Park today, the wind is winding itself around me and pushing my thoughts. I thought, why not delve into the great religions of the world and see what they have to say about luck. I would contact a priest, a rabbi, a Buddhist monk, a learned Mullah, and dip into their wisdom. I'd scale it down to the pure luck, the lottery type. None of that prepared luck which is the easy part. No, the one where a petty criminal wins 10 million dollars and doesn't deserve it at all. I struck it lucky with my first call.

I arrived at the Brompton Oratory on a cold and rainy spring day. The Oratory is <u>the</u> Catholic Church in London. If you're thinking about marrying your daughter off and you're Catholic this is the place. I am directed to a building behind the church that I have never noticed before and with my heart pounding I knock on the imposing doors. A gruff little man answers the door, "Are you here for confession?"

"No, well, actually," I stumble around, "I'd just like to talk to one of the priests please." I am led to a small room furnished with table and two chairs, a tall friendly priest walks in, eyes twinkling he invites me to sit down.

"What can I do for you?"

"Father, I am writing a book and I want to know the Church's position on luck." I look away afraid to see his reaction. But he warms to the subject.

"Luck, well let me think, yes. I would say, Thomas Aquinas has mentioned it and Dante, of course."

Luck has come down to us from the goddess Fortuna, an earlier deity taken from the Greek goddess Tyche. Fortuna was worshipped both in Greece and Italy, more particularly in Rome where she was considered as the goddess of good luck, success and every kind of prosperity; newly married women dedicated their maiden garments to the two temples built for her. The Ancient Romans believed that Rome was an exceptionally lucky place and was blessed by the Gods. In the story related by Plutarch it was said that on entering Rome Fortuna put off her wings and shoes and threw away the globe, as she intended to take up her permanent home among the Romans.

In early times, Fortuna was shown perpetually turning the wheel of transformation, which marked the heavenly seasons and human fate. In the medieval world, Fortuna's symbols of fertility and change were transformed into icons of luck. Her wheel became part of roulette ('little wheel'), a popular carnival game during the Middle Ages. Fortuna was reborn as Lady Luck.

In one way one could say that all religion was based on wanting better luck and wanting guidance for the future. To try to discover the will of God the Jews also had their oracles in their sanctuaries in Jerusalem. On certain occasions when the priest wanted to consult Yahweh he tried, through oracles, to divine the future. The Jews saw these statues as just idols, lights along the way. But people endowed these idols with luck. People still pray to various saints trying to win over luck to their side. "You know, things have not changed very much," the priest continued, "A very religious woman came to me yesterday. She told me if she went more to communion she thought she would be luckier. I told her this had nothing to do with her luck. She was very disappointed." He paused, "In our faith one would say that God controls everything but the secondary events in life are left to chance. In a sense he has consigned these events to heavenly roulette. Of course, it has no moral significance. Perfectly evil people have had good luck visit them. One must always remember the temporal rewards of this world are always taken away at the end and one never knows if having good luck just means being healthy and having nice children."

"Thank you so much for helping me," I say.

"I am presently reading the Koran," he adds. "In the Moslem religion all is arranged by God, it is all in Allah's hands, there's no room for pure chance."

I turn to him, "thank you again for your time and may luck be with you." I just couldn't help it ....

19.

Down on one's Luck

*'Some people are so fond of ill luck
that they run half-way to met it.'
(Jerrold, Douglas 1803-1857)*

It gets worse. Karl is out of jail for a few months on parole before he goes back in for four years! He has visited Marie-Louise's sick and dying mother, who, of course, is not speaking to Marie-Louise. All slick and smooth, he has helped her mother to make hospital arrangements for herself and, of course, visited her lawyers and bankers with her. How caring, how human except he has helped her mother to reorganize her last will and testament. It looks like he is now the executor of Marie-Louise's family fortune. He wins. Total control over family or has he pushed his luck too far?

"I'm not lucky,," Marie-Louise screams into the phone. "You better write that book about luck, for everything hangs on luck. Besides, Karl wrapping up my mother, he has won another case against me in the courts."

"Of course, when you're really not lucky there is always revenge to even out the score," I suggest.

"What am I doing wrong?"

I answer, "unfortunately good and bad luck often falls at random and the best thing to do, as Kipling said, is to treat the two impostors just the same. In the end, what matters is not what you do when you're lucky, it's what you do in spite of it. And you must look at this situation as an exciting challenge."

"My dear friend, that's easy for you to say, all that positive thinking, but I'm desperate, I've got bills to pay and I think my family fortune has just been taken out of my hands. I must frighten him, break his arms, some bones, no, his legs so he can't walk ..."

Karl, your luck may be running out. Everyone has his or her limits. Beware out there, women and men have their limits and people who have been passive all their life and have accepted being manipulated go over the top with revenge. The papers are full of women and men shooting their nearest and dearest and their teachers and bosses. On top of everything, Marie-Louise's brother has arrived, unfortunately not to help her out, but to gather information on what she is up to. Marie-Louise thinks he is there to see Karl, another person Karl has sucked into his vortex for he has also lent Karl money. Karl has just written to her from the South of France "Sorry, no money, honey". Nice. Families and friends are connected together in circles of energy and this circle is definitely lopsided, all will pay till it's set right again.

Remember,

Luck has nothing to do with Morality.

20

How to Avoid Bad Luck

These tried and true methods of avoiding bad luck have come down to us through the centuries.

Avoid The Number 13

The number 13 is universally considered bad luck. It is tied up with devils and witches and black magic. Plus, Jesus' crucifixion took place on Friday the thirteenth and the last dinner comprised 12 apostles and Jesus. Not a good number.

To this day, in most countries, the number 13 is avoided in street numbers, office buildings, and no one would dare to plan an event on Friday the thirteenth. I wonder whether America was blessed or cursed starting off with its original 13 colonies. It didn't bother the Americans who designed the Great Seal on the back of the dollar bill in 1935, thirteen stars, thirteen stripes, thirteen steps. and the Bald Eagle is holding thirteen arrows and thirteen leaves. The exception!

Don't Break A Mirror

Breaking a mirror will bring you seven years of bad luck. Everyone knows this. If you break a mirror, get rid of the broken glass immediately to carry away any trace of bad luck. Mirrors in olden days were believed to catch the soul of someone who looked too long into it. Even today, when someone dies in the Jewish religion, the mirror is covered to prevent the soul from being trapped in the mirror between this and the next world.

Black Cats

Black cats can bring you good or bad luck depending on which country you are in. But one thing you don't want is it crossing your path, except if you're in England where it means good luck.

Don't Walk Under A Ladder

The origin of ladder superstitions dates back to the belief in the sanctity of the trinity as a potent force against the workings of evil. When a ladder is placed against a wall, it forms a natural triangle. It is a symbol of the Holy Trinity or the Holy Family. To pass through this mystical space unbalances the three-pronged balance of power, causing the guardian spirits to take offense.

Evil Eye

Since early times, people were known to have the evil eye. When they looked at you bad things would happen. To protect yourself against these people, one should carry an amulet or outstare them or quickly avert your eyes and walk away from them.

Knock On Wood Three Times

Knocking on wood three times gives you a double bonus. You are using the powerful forces of the number three and acknowledging the power of trees where the ancient gods lived. It is said that knocking on wood is symbolically knocking on the door to heaven.

Cross Your Middle Fingers For Good Luck

As we all know, crossing your fingers behind your back nullifies white lies. Held in front of you it means a wish of good luck and averting disaster. Usually, this is done in a light-hearted manner but underneath this gesture stands the powerful symbol of the cross. The point of the center of your crossed fingers will always be regarded as a profound and effecting focal point pulsating with protection and luck.

Throw Some Salt Over Your Left Shoulder

Salt has always been an extremely valuable commodity equated with gold. Soldiers were once paid in salt. Ancient civilizations from Greece to Mexico had designated their goddesses to salt. So, the spilling of salt was considered bad luck due to its great value. Why throw salt over your left shoulder? Early man believed good spirits rested on your right side and the evil one on your left. To soothe the evil spirit one tossed salt over one's left shoulder.

Confuse The Gods

If things are going well, never admit it or say it. The Ancient Greeks believed strongly in this. Don't brag or ever think you are above the Gods. They called this 'hubris'. History is scattered with people who thought they were superhuman and fell to the bottom. Always complain a bit how things could be a bit better.

21

Charmed Luck

"To charm someone is to make someone feel special using only the force of your words and presence. Charm falls into the world of magic and those who have this magnetic appeal can make their luck."

There is a way you can come in to luck through the backdoor. You can charm your way into luck.

In all the great philosophical conversations on chance no one, as far as I know, has discussed the effects of charm and its ability to change lives. Charm is a talent. A powerful talent. Most often given at birth in the genetic bundle of goodies (one would say that's luck to start with) as a gift. Somewhat similar to the gift of writing, or singing. But writing and singing will be nurtured in the years ahead with much practice and dedication. Great natural charm does not have to be worked at; it just exists. I think of the many confidence men and women able to charm people out of all their earthly possessions, leaving the general population panting, in shock, emotionally shattered, broke and broken, and still not being able to hate these people who have used them for their own gain, so powerful is this gift of charm.

Our Karl has that natural charm. Yes, we haven't until now mentioned his weapon. He had used his charm to win over and seduce everyone up till now. Yes, he was able to get the women he wanted, the money he wanted and the lifestyle he wanted. God, was he lucky! His luck came rushing to him, easily, quickly, fun loving, skipping, running on rivers of Champagne, but here it comes. Luck will not stay with you forever. Unfortunate, but true. Everything in the world goes in streaks, some larger than others. It's truly a real phenomenon and you can see it everywhere, in stock markets, at the gambling table, in people's lives. Sometimes it's just great for a while, a wave of good things, and then it just stops. And once it goes bad, it also seems to stay bad for longer. The folk wisdom of bad things happening in threes, is also true. There's even a scientific theory on it called 'The Complexity Theory' that supports this age-old saying. Bad things cluster and last a while longer. So, when this streak or period of good luck is experienced it must be realized and when it's gone you have to live again like it never happened to you and continue to appreciate what you have at the moment. But no one is willing to let that good streak run away from them without a fight. People try to re-invent what they think worked for them before. Well, it doesn't work. Chinese astrology would say it was a certain field of time and that time was set up for the possibilities that happened to you, and they were realized. You must move on. Karl's luck had run out. When it turned against him and ebbed away, he fought harder and harder to catch it and fell into the pattern of a reckless gambler who in the end out of desperation bets everything and loses everything. You must walk away from the table when the odds go against you. And now Karl is in jail.

I must add, I was surrounded for a certain time in my life with this charm, my dear friend Claudine, a charmer par excellence and my husband. Both are French and masters of calculated charm. God, when those two got together my jaw just dropped. Ah! The French! Now, that's a whole country of calculated charmeurs using their intelligence and sexual wiles to attain what they want. It's a fatal mixture. Luckily the French, men and women, are equipped to play this calculated game. Outsiders beware! Both of my charmeurs had attained the goals they had set out for. Claudine naturally got her rich, famous husband in marriage, my husband attained great success in his business. Often with charmeurs, people around them— children, partners, friends—who are caught in their web wake up one day as from a dream to see that these charmeurs are really interested only in themselves. And while charming and soothing everyone around them into a false assumption that they are loving and caring, they are relentlessly pursuing their own goal. I have seen charmers turn this magnetic charm on and off like a water faucet. Where one moment there were smiles, soft voices, spreading excitement and sexual brightness, the next moment, behind this mask, a cold, hard mind would surface when the victim had left. A superficial charm, but powerful. Behind my husband's charm was an emptiness, huge holes of space. It frightened me. I didn't understand it. This charming, incredibly convincing man could charm yours truly (who knew better), tough Swiss Bankers and shrewd hard businessmen to give him exactly what he wanted. "Stay with me," he implied, "I hold the promise of excitement, money, power." It was the same with my girlfriend. All charming women are cut from the classic courtesan mould. Very emotional, sexual, feminine in every way, they exude a pulsating charm. Enjoy their net of magic, behind them is another person.

I even thought at one point that their power of seduction was in their voices. Have you ever noticed that the real charmers you meet have silken voices? It must set up a certain resonance that makes the molecules in your body feel good and you are charmed. There is a power in sound and it is known that a certain juxtaposition of musical notes as in a Mozart piano concerto can accelerate one's intelligence and reasoning skills. Why can it not be a certain sound, which raises a feel good factor in other people?

If you find you have a nice speaking voice you must develop this ability to use your voice and words to weave a spell around people. A magic rush of words, flattering your victims, deprecating yourself with a hint of sexual desire always happening at the edges. With you around, their world sparkles a little bit more. People feel they are more interesting, cleverer. You are someone who has recognized their own special qualities. I once was charmed off my feet by a terribly unattractive young man who, with the most apologetic manner and excruciating politeness, made me feel like a queen. This approach really does work for men and for women. Try it!

Let's take 1996 and America's charmer, OJ Simpson—a man with buckets of charm and athletic prowess was up for murder. In case you were on the moon at that time, OJ Simpson, America's super sports hero, had been charged with killing his wife and a friend of hers. Despite the evidence the prosecution brought against him, OJ Simpson' attorney, Cochran was able to convince the jury and America that he was not guilty of murder. How could such a charming, good-looking, talented sportsman possibly be accused of committing something as ugly as that? What would have been the verdict, I wonder, had he been ugly, fat, badly dressed with tiny sneaky eyes, balding and charmless? Well, just remember that charm has nothing to do with intelligence, it falls into that world of magic. The ability to bewitch someone. It originates from ancient times when there was no other reasonable explanation. It still applies.

Of course, I have my own theory what charm really is. It goes something like this. Each one of us, uniquely, reflects the energy of the world around us. We are like prisms of light sending out our beams to everything around us. We just can't see it and each one of us reflects and sends it in our own way. Our charmeurs produce a higher resonance of magnetic energy, which strongly pulls whatever they want in their direction. Once they are aware of this force, they can control it for this force can go beyond the immediate object or emotion. If it's strong enough it extends to whole nations. It can inspire loyalty and enthusiasm. It is called a "charismatic personality."

Great Charmers of Our Time

Princess Di

My ex-husband

Probably your last lover
who ripped your heart out
and left you suddenly
with no explanation.

The all time political charmer was JF Kennedy

Sean Connery

Nations of people are charming or not

Germanic countries: charm takes a back seat. I'm still trying
to figure out what's in the front seat.

America: due to its mix of cultures has much charm.
Southern charm, Latin charm, Afro-American charm, even
Homer Simpson on his good days has charm. But, for my taste,
there are too many honest, dull, health-conscious, politically
correct folks.

Ireland: is a land of charmers. Go there to take lessons.

France: is the place to be for learning a thing or two about
sexual, calculated charm.

Italy" who can resist the natural charm of an Italian man
when he wants you.

22.

Gamblers' Luck

*'I am the game of dice, I am the Self
seated in the heart of Beings. I am the
Beginning and the Middle and the End of
all Beings. I am Vishnu, the Beaming Sun
among shining bodies'*
said by the God Krishna in the Bhagavad-Gita.

The first time I gambled was on holiday. My father and I had left my mother upstairs in our hotel room and had wandered down to the gambling casino of a San Juan Hotel. We were swept over to a table in the corner where to my wide-eyed amazement everyone seemed to be bathed in an extra bright light. Big American men with huge gold watches, stomachs tumbling over onto the crap table were screaming so loud the air around them quivered. The table was hot. We inched our way in, and having beginners' luck, had placed our money on the number seven. What followed was the longest winning role of sevens in a row that I have ever seen. (On an opening role of seven you win your bet.) Well, my personality changed. Out went the shy young student, in came my other self until then hidden— passionate, intense, screaming. I was the game; I was one with everyone there. I cannot exactly explain now that feeling I had but I remember I felt so joyful, so childlike. It is a rush that positively makes you giddy with happiness. I remember my father and I stuffing our pockets with money like kids with big smiles on our faces as we left the casino. I can see how nations have an uneasy truce with gambling. Look at the Lottery. Name me one person who doesn't buy a ticket. The lottery winnings have helped to build towns, bridges, and schools all over the world since the inception in 1466 in Belgium to raise funds for the poor citizens of Bruges. In 1746, Columbia was founded on luck; a New York Lottery raised money to found this American University.

People will and have gambled away their fortunes, their wives, all their possessions, and even their lives just for that feeling of living intensely for a moment in time. I have read that North American Indians gamble for all their possessions, wives, children, horses, everything. They come back from the gambling ground with nothing but their lives. And in Europe, lands and possessions have easily slipped out of aristocratic hands for the intense moments of a game of cards with everything at stake.

If one ranks emotional intensity as the most important thing in life as the primitive mind does, then gambling with dice takes the top position. Dice have their own story. Used throughout history to tell peoples' fortunes. Wise men would roll them and interpret dreams and future events by the numbers rolled. Dice actually only became a proper game in the 18th Century. It has been passionately played ever since. For with dice there is a connection, a psychic energy and the act of gambling. When the spirit of the unconscious gambles, which we were doing around the table, one creates fate even if it's for a few brief fleeting moments because its creation is a synchronistic phenomenon. You have unconsciously created a run of luck. All of us at that table created a movement in time, a creative act, where we willed psychically and physically those rolling dice to win. Nowhere else does the physical and mental act show so clearly the creative act where everything comes together than a run of luck in dice. We stood rooted to the spot surrounded by a wall of screaming voices enveloping us. All minds willing together and then at one point the energy broke and then it was over. The silence returned and my conscious mind returned, the devious, rational part came rushing in. Next time, I will really know how to play the game the right way, I thought. I will beat the odds again. Giggling and laughing we left the tables. I have never recaptured that wondrous feeling again. Perhaps it has to do with the first time of anything and in Europe gambling is a quiet affair, all hushed voices and the clipped correct voices of the French croupiers. But I think you need the power of sound, it creates vibrations. It's an important element that goes with the spirit of the unconscious at a moment in time. All together it makes a synchronistic event. It's not a predictable act but a creative act in time.

Of course, I am not the first one to think there might be a way to beat the odds in gambling. There is a calculus of probability and it was invented by two Frenchmen, the mathematician and philosopher Blaise Pascal, and Pierre de Fermat, considered one of the greatest mathematicians of all time. A gambler wrote to Pascal and asked him for a system of gambling so he could win. Pascal became mathematically interested and started a correspondence with Fermat about it. No one knows who had the idea first but between them they discovered the calculus of probability. Thus, mathematics was recognized as the determining factor in gambling.

Professional gamblers make up their own mathematical systems to beat the system and gifted mathematicians who also use algebraic means to describe the probabilities of a sequence of events and have worked out their own unique gambling systems. These men are not wanted at the tables in Las Vegas. As soon as the Casino operators catch on they are asked to leave.

Most games played are a mixture of chance and calculation. You use your intelligence to a certain extent but there is always the law of probabilities involved. The odds in horse racing are generally seven or eight to one, in dice, thirty-five to one, and in a lottery 500,000 to one. In games of pure chance, betting on sports matches or flipping coins the odds are 50 to 50. Luck and gambling have always been thought of together. In the ritual of play, one makes room for chance to come in and capriciously throw some money your way. But you must know when to leave the table.

Insurances gamble with chance constantly with calculations and statistics. They eliminate chance in order to arrive at the average American driver with his average security. Naturally, that can't cover everything. Chance still plays tricks and under English law, even officially in the courts, chance, which is not foreseen by the insurance companies, is called an Act of God. That is the official term. Chance is an Act of God! What a way to get out of paying people some extra money. But miscalculations in chance can bring down an insurance company. Our modern day fiasco at Lloyd's of London has left the wealthy participants reeling from their debts they must cover for the unforeseen calamities that Lloyd's suffered from.

23

Chance, Synchronicity, Seriality

'Chance favours the prepared mind.'
Louis Pasteur

Now luck falls under the net of Chance. Each chance that comes our way we accept or reject. The 'chance meeting'. 'Take a chance'. Strangely enough, chance has occupied only a few of our great Western thinkers. But the chance meeting or occurrence has puzzled man since the dawn of mythology.

Paul Kammerer

One of those brilliant thinkers interested in chance was Paul Kammerer, a Viennese biologist. Kammerer believed in the significance of apparent coincidences. He was fascinated by coincidences and from the age of twenty kept an accurate extensive logbook on his observations. He spent hours on trains, public areas, and parks, just observing people. He would note down the numbers of people that strolled by in both directions, classifying them by sex, age, and dress. Then, he would analyze his findings. His tables showed that on every parameter a typical clustering phenomenon familiar to statisticians, gamblers and insurance companies came up.

Unfortunately, he was accused of faking his results (Arthur Koestler, later writing his biography found out that it was not true) and committed suicide in 1926 at the young age of forty-five. Kammerer published his theory in a book called "Das

Gesetz der Serie". In it he defined his concept of 'seriality' as the concurrence in space or recurrence in time of meaningfully, but not causally connected events. Kammerer sought to prove that coincidences, whether they come singly, or in a series are manifestations of a universal principle in nature, which operates independently from physical causation. He was particularly interested in temporal series of recurrent events; these he regarded as cyclic processes, which propagate themselves like waves along the time axis of the space-time continuum. He regarded single coincidences as merely tips of the iceberg, which happens to catch the eye, an isolated coincidence while the troughs remain unnoticed. The cycles may be caused by causal factors (i.e. planetary motion) or patterned by seriality—as the lucky runs of gamblers. But there is a force, which acts selectively on form and function to bring similar configurations together in space and time: it correlates by affinity. It functions outside the known laws of physics. This a-causal agency intrudes into the causal order of things. In space it produces concurrent events related by affinity, in time, similarly related series. "Thus one arrives at the image of a world-mosaic or cosmic kaleidoscope which in spite of constant shuffling and rearrangements also takes care of bringing like and like together."

The first half of his book contains exactly one hundred selected samples of coincidental series classified in a biologists meticulous manner. There is a typology of non-causal concurrence related to numbers, names, and situations. At the end of the first classificatory part of the book, Kammerer concludes: "So far we have been concerned with the factual manifestations of recurrent series, without attempting an explanation. We have found that the recurrence of identical or similar data in contiguous areas of space or time is a simple empirical fact which has to be accepted and which cannot be explained by coincidences, or rather, which makes coincidence rule to such an extent that the concept of coincidence itself is negated." After this, he devotes a chapter to previous theories of periodicity, from Pythagorean's magic seven to Goethe's revolving circles of good and bad days, up to Freud who believed in cycles of twenty-three and twenty-seven days which combine to produce the data of significant events. In the second part of the book, Kammerer develops his central idea that co-existent with causality there is an a-causal principle active in the universe which tends towards unity.

One chapter deals with the Morphology of Series which are classified according to their 'order' (the number of successive coincidences), their power (number of parallel coincidences), and their parameters (number of shared attributes). Some of the other chapters in the book cover physics and other tantalizing flashes of intuition. At the end of the book, Kammerer states his belief that Seriality is "ubiquitous and continuous in life, nature and cosmos. It is the umbilical cord that connects thought, feeling, science and art with the womb of the universe which gave birth to them."

Carl G Jung

Carl G Jung, the Swiss psychologist, dedicated many years of his life to the study of chance. Jung was convinced that there was some linking process at work in the universe, collaboration between the human psyche and the external world that transcended established laws of physics.

Jung's idea was based on the age-old wisdom of antiquity that the constellations of the planets governed man's character and destiny that everything hangs together, not by mechanical causes but by hidden affinities. In the Ancient world, there was no room for coincidences. The doctrine of the 'sympathy of all things' can be traced all the way back to Hippocrates. There is one common flow, one common breathing, all things are in sympathy. This theme also runs through the teachings of Taoism and Buddhism and is the foundation for magic, astrology, and alchemy. This concept held up until the Renaissance where it completely vanished with the rise of the physical sciences.

Contemporary physicists have now come round full circle and agree it is impossible to separate any part of the universe from the rest. The old Newtonian world of the hard indestructible atom is gone and an ever-changing energy is in its place.

According to Jung, all divinatory practices from looking at tea leaves to the complicated oracular methods of the I Ching are based on the idea that random events are minor mysteries, which can be used as pointers towards the one central mystery. Thus, his Synchronicity and Kammerer's Seriality are modern derivatives of the archetypal belief in the fundamental unity of all things, transcending mechanical causality. Jung's essay on Synchronicity published in 1952 was partly based on Kammerer's book *Das Gesetz der Serie* published in 1919. Jung defined synchronicity as the "simultaneous occurrence of two or more meaningfully but not causally connected events." The agents of synchronicity are found in what he called the archetypes of the human psyche. Just as human beings share certain genetic features they also have certain psychological material, archetypes in common. These appear in the unconscious mind as symbols such as a tree, a father, and the sun. They hold a certain relevance or meaning for the person. These archetypes become conscious to us only in dreams, slips of the tongue, reveries. They are symbols. They are not conceived by the conscious mind but arise from the 'collective unconscious'. This unconscious mind functions outside the physical framework of space-time and the 'meaningful coincidences' rest on this archetypal foundation. These archetypes serve as psychic catalysts that manifest in the physical world. Jung defined synchronistic events as acts of creation. It rests on the simultaneous occurrence of two different psychic states. One of them is the normal probable state and the other, the critical experience, is the one that cannot be derived causally from the first. Modern physicists agree with Jung's act of creation for they also think there is in the world, in which we live, a place where from time to time, new things are created. This synchronistic event would be one of these acts of creation where psychic energy is released and sets up a flow that involves the field of people around one. This manifestation can be the famous coincidences that we all have experienced. Thinking about someone, then shortly afterwards bumping into them.

Modern science has a parallel to this mystical concept of 'this oneness' or Jung's modern version of it. It is that 'all is energy'. It is based on the integrative powers of all living matter.

Jung coined the term *Synchronicity*. When asked why he used the word synchronicity, he responded by defining it as the seemingly accidental meeting of two unrelated causal chains in a coincidental event. "... [T]his falling together in time is a kind of simultaneousness. Because of this quality of simultaneousness I have picked on the term "synchronicity" to designate a hypothetical factor equal in rank to causality as a principle of explanation."

Jung takes the coincidence of events in space and time as meaning something more than mere chance; namely it is a peculiar interdependence of objective events among themselves and with the subjective (psychic) states of the observer or observers.

Wolfgang Pauli

Wolfgang Pauli, the noted Nobel-Prize winning physicist, also gave much thought to this subject. He felt that apparent coincidences were the visible traces of untraceable acausal principles in the Universe. He collaborated with CG Jung on their famous joint essay: Synchronicity: An Acausal Connecting Principle.

Wolfgang Pauli was the discoverer of the Exclusion Principle, a purely mathematical construct that stated that "any one of the planetary orbits inside an atom can only be occupied by one electron at a time. If it were not so, chaos would result and the atom would collapse." It was a mathematical symmetry imposed upon the basic equations of nature and without his theory the quantum theory would not have held up. Pauli shared Kammerer's and Jung's belief in non-causal non-physical factors operating in the Universe. Was not his own Exclusion Principle acting like a force, though it is not a force? Pauli probably had a more profound insight than most of his colleagues into the limitations of science. Like Jung he was haunted all his life by poltergeist-like phenomena. When he was fifty and a Nobel Laureate, he wrote a penetrating study on science and mysticism, as reflected by the ideas of Johannes Kepler, who was both a mystic and the founder of modern astronomy. Pauli's revolutionary proposal was to extend the concept of non-causal events from the world of the microcosms, where its legitimacy was recognized, to the world of the macrocosms.

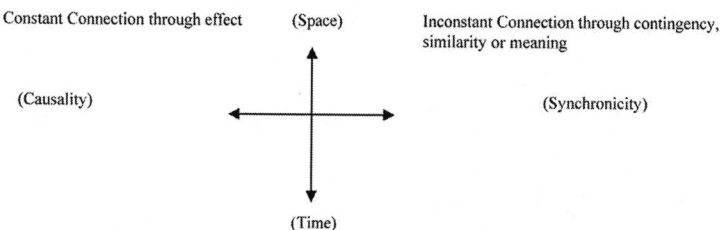

At some point, Jung and Pauli managed to work together and agree on the above diagram. It must have been a fascinating exercise for the both of them. They used the triad of classical physics — space, time, and causality and added the synchronicity factor, which made it a tetrad, a quaternion, which makes possible a whole new judgement. Jung unfortunately offers no concrete explanation on how the schema is meant to work. I leave it up to you out there to interpret it.

One wonders what would have happened if Pauli could have pushed out into black holes and time running backward utilizing Jung's psychological thoughts.

Arthur Koestler

The well-known English writer, Arthur Koestler, was also interested in coincidences. He wrote several books about Chance. Koestler's contribution was to try and base coincidence on a more scientific basis. He decided to assemble as large a database as possible of coincidences to give a higher quality of evidence. His classification of the different kinds of luck and the elements involved has become a classic. Koestler found the terms 'Seriality' and 'Synchronicity' awkward terms with their misplaced emphasis on time alone. He preferred to substitute them instead with the expression 'confluential events'. Confluential events would be acausal manifestations of the Integrative Tendency, a universal principle that includes a-causal phenomena. Koestler defined it as 'increasing order', a higher form of unity in a more complex variety. He gave as an idea 'the psycho-kinetic effects on rolling dice', and other paranormal a-causal phenomena. What lends them significance is that they give the impression of being causally connected, though they demonstrably are not; the dice seem to be manipulated by the experimenter's or gambler's will. The integrative potentials of life seem to include the capacity of producing pseudo—causal effects.

There was a remarkable series of experiments pertaining to this manipulation of outside objects through one's will. It was performed by one of Britain's most respected neurophysiologists, Dr W Grey Walter. In his 1969 Eddington Memorial lecture, he reported that "harnessed to an electric machine, by an effort of will, one can influence external events without movement or overt action through the impalpable electric surges of one's own brain. This effort "requires a peculiar state of concentration, a paradoxical compound of detachment and excitement." His experiments bordered on what we call ESP using our mental will to make something happen. To exert influence over the outer world in this way is still unfamiliar to us. Spontaneous paranormal ESP it seems is always bound up with some self-transcending type of motion. If we repeat something one time too many we get bored and it declines. In ESP sittings, there is a characteristic falling off in the number of 'hits' on the score sheet. This decline effect is regarded as an additional proof for the reality of 'Beginner's Luck'. It falls under our inability to control the unconscious processes underlying our ESP. Our initial excitement causes something to happen but it is difficult to replicate it again. According to Grey Walter, to influence outside events our readiness wave (our electrical brain waves) can attain sufficient strength if the subject is in a state described as a paradoxical compound of detachment and excitement.

Professor HH Price adds an interesting suggestion regarding the apparent capriciousness of ESP. "It looks as if telepathically received impressions have some difficulty in crossing the threshold and manifesting themselves in consciousness. There seems to be some barrier or repressive mechanism which tends to shut them out from consciousness, a barrier which is rather difficult to pass, and they make use of all sorts of devices for overcoming it." Price suggests that automatic speech or writing dreams, hallucinations and many of our everyday thoughts and emotions are telepathic, or partly telepathic, in origin, but mixed up with other mental contents and are distorted crossing the threshold of consciousness.

Adrian Dobbs comments on Prices thoughts: "This is a very interesting passage. It evokes the picture of either the mind or the brain as containing an assemblage of selective filters, designed to cut out unwanted signals on neighbouring frequencies, some of which get through in a distorted form, just as in ordinary radio reception."

Since Koestler`s death, his Foundation has continued to promote research into the areas of amazing coincidences and has continued to receive accounts of synchronistic occurrences from around the world.

Koestler's Chart on Luck

Good Luck

Classification	The Result of	Elements involved	Personality traits you need
Chance 1 "Blind" Luck	An accident	Chance happenings and nothing is directly attributable to you, the recipient	None
Chance 2 The Kettering Principle	General exploratory behaviour	Chance favours those in motion. Events are brought together to form "happy accidents" when you diffusely apply energies in typically nonspecific motions	Curiosity about many things, persistence, willingness to experiment and to explore
Chance 3 The Pasteur	Sagacity	Chance favours the prepared mind. Receptivity from past experience permits you to discern a new fact or perceive ideas in a new relationship	A background of knowledge based on abilities to , observe remember and quickly form significant new associations
Chance 4 The Disraeli	Personalised action	Chance favours the individualised action. Fortuitous events occur when you behave - in ways that are highly distinctive of you as a person	Distinctive hobbies, personal lifestyles, and activities peculiar to you, especially when they operate in domains seemingly far from the area of discovery.

ESP

But, let's go even a step backwards from synchronistic events or blocked thoughts. What made you think of going to the store where you bumped into that long lost friend of yours? Or what made you think of a friend and then two minutes later he called you on the phone? Why did you decide to think that? Well, one thing is clear, we really are not set up to think why did we think that way but the late Professor Broad wrote an article in philosophy that might shed some light on this. "If paranormal cognition and paranormal causation are facts, then it is quite likely that they are not confined to those very rare occasions on which they either manifest themselves sporadically in a spectacular way, or to those very special conditions in which their presence can be experimentally established. They may well be continually operating in the background of our normal lives. Our understanding of, and our misunderstandings with, our fellow men (and women), our general emotional mood on certain occasions, the ideas which suddenly arise in our minds without any obvious introspectable cause, our unaccountable immediate emotional reactions towards certain persons, ... and so on, all these may be in part determined by paranormal cognition and paranormal causal influences."

But, to end this chapter let's take the contrarian view. I refer to two renowned Harvard University scientistis who, after a decade of research, are adamant that there are no extraordinary forces outside the realm of science which are acting to produce these coincidences. Their findings show that coincidences are not so incredible. For instance, there need to be only twenty-three people in a room for it to be likely that two of them will share the same birthday.

24.

Clusters

There is a tendency for events to happen together. In a certain spirit of time certain questions and psychological problems are constellated. Then several people have the same questions and come up with the same results. It's in the air. There seem to be two types of clusters, serial clusterings, which are purely mechanical, and synchronicities, which imply that the mind itself has some influence over the laws of nature. These clusters often run in threes; the old wives tale is true. It's a natural phenomenon, even modern-day science agrees. It runs in streaks and then Bam!

Which brings me back to Marie-Louise. She has run away from Zürich. The Cluster of events has become too overwhelming. Everything, and I mean everything, is happening at the same time (negatively, of course). It's like the end of this part of her life before she can start again. I hope. The Lausanne Tribunal (behind closed doors) has definitely decided that Karl is mucho, mucho guilty and has sentenced him to another five years. Marie-Louise, who up till now had been living with him, has now developed a tumor. I've often seen this happen. Women, after going through a rough patch in their marriage, whisper to me they are so happy they stayed with their husbands. I wait two minutes for the rest: in lowered tones they tell me how well they've gotten over their chemotherapy treatments. The distorted bodily reaction to a distorted pattern in a stress-filled moment in time. So we've got Karl ready to go back into jail, with no alimony payments ahead for Marie-Louise, who is virtually penniless, her name destroyed, a tumor in her stomach and her mother sick and dying in the local hospital. God, talk about clusters.

25.

Force of Destiny in Luck

While I was discussing with my son, we whizzed into Rymans to buy a typewriter. Yes, a typewriter. I have decided the computer has a place in my life, but I must be the mistress of what I write. I must touch the paper, have the push and pull of the keys, the noise. Simply said, the interaction gives me pleasure.

No worrying about computer viruses for me. "So, Julian, what do you think luck is?" I know my son's answer, getting lucky with some girl, but I'm curious what an 18-year-old will answer. Peoples' answers have started falling into two camps. Either they say life is chaos and luck falls by accident or one has a destiny, a karma and luck comes to you because you and your destiny have set yourself up to receive it. I ask again pushing away his daydreams. Well, what do you think? I don't really know, he hedges. Well, at that age it's a reasonable answer. The day before we had attended a psychic fair/workshop in London where a Canadian Indian had mesmerized all of us with his thoughts about life and how he was here to help us poor old white folks get it right with mother earth. I wish I'd asked him what Indians think about luck. I did, however, get a chance to talk to Dr Richard Lawrence who is the Director of the Aetherius Society, a College of spiritual sciences. They teach metaphysics, a branch of philosophy that deals with explaining the nature of being or reality, which comprises ontology, cosmology and epistemology. They also give courses in psychic development, yoga and healing. Well, after a rather interesting exchange of views on my subject, I decided to pick up his book and see in depth what he thinks about destiny. I quote:

"Although people may refute the idea that there is an overall destiny factor governing life and choose to believe in a completely haphazard existence based on chance, their behavior would suggest otherwise. It is amazing, for example, just how many people are superstitious in one way or another. Although they may scoff at superstition, they nevertheless will not walk under a ladder, for example.

There is a fascination with the whole subject of chance. Millions of people around the world gamble in one way or another on the premise that it might be their lucky day. I am referring here not just to those who place bets, for the financial markets are also a source of speculation and gambling. Even though people might strongly deny it, a part of them believes that there is a destiny at work in life, and by gambling they are banking on it working in their favour.

After I had been using the crystal ball for some time and had given hundreds of readings with it, I began to realize that you could read almost anything on which you choose to see the signs of destiny imprinted. The only proviso is that you must be in the correct psychic condition when you do it. I suppose the principle behind all systems is really exactly the same, whether it is the runes or reading car number-plates. Throwing coins for the purpose of the I Ching or picking cards for the Tarot are apparently haphazard, but they rest on the principle that nothing happens by chance. With the Tarot and the I Ching you can make more of a ritual out of it, but it is still based on a pattern of destiny being reflected in procedures apparently based on pure chance.

The ancient Romans and Greeks were particularly expert at reading the signs of life through weather portents and other methods. Indeed, in certain cases major military decisions were heavily influenced by this type of reading, and at one time very few Roman generals would consider going to war without first consulting an oracle or a seer. After practising divination for a while you do start to realize that there is another superhuman factor at work.

All these systems conform to this mysterious force of destiny—from this all the predictions and other evaluations are made. It is therefore vital to gain a deeper understanding of what exactly destiny is and how it works out in people's lives. As a psychic you are able to help others use their forces of destiny that are affecting their lives to the best possible advantage. Just as mind energy travels in wave motions, so do certain aspects of destiny flow in cycles. There is a good time to do certain things and a time to be wary of certain trends, influences and patterns of behavior. A time to sow and a time to reap. We are all really aware of this knowledge, but somehow we don't trust it or have not been able to place it in our lives properly."

26.

Don't count on Luck in a Divorce

Napoleon I (1769-1821)
'Has he luck?' Habitually asked to assess a man's probable practical value.

I need a lawyer, not just a good lawyer, a lucky lawyer. Someone who wins cases. I have been divorced for a year. Now, my ex-husband sells his company and pockets for himself a small fortune, making him one of the richest men in Switzerland. Doesn't this sound familiar? Husband bankrupt at divorce, one year later they pop up with house in south of France and a condo in Aspen. Well, even in the inner workings of the Swiss banking world this amount raises eyebrows. I want a slice of this large fortune, of what you might call his good luck. There's money to be made with a good lawyer. Luckily, I'm not one of those women who can't find the missing bank accounts which have been conveniently shipped offshore. No, this is public domain; also it's become the public domain in the world of gossip. Now when I walk into any restaurant eyes look up to me, then away and in whispered voices they ask each other, "Did she get any of it? Will his new girlfriend get any of it?" Or like my friend says, "Your son, when he grows up, will have any blond girl he wants."

Today, my appointment is with a top international Swiss lawyer who's also a Colonel in the Swiss Army. Perfect! I told my Swiss banker we had to increase my positions, which is financespeak for increasing the money in my portfolio, so he has contacted his old army buddy, Heinrich Stutze.

Herr Stutze is seated in front of an enormous flag that covers the whole wall of his office. I've never seen this flag before and wonder if I've walked into some Polynesian Embassy. It is a summer day, beginning of April, a light breeze ruffles through this comfortably lived in office. Most of the older generation Swiss have these nice human rooms. Go into one of the young yuppie law offices, it's all modern paintings, white walls, skinny sleek furniture and hungry mouths. They look at the clocks on the walls. The older Swiss lawyers are pretty content by the time they reach their mid-fifties.

"I don't take new clients, Frau Alleno, but due to Herr Meier asking me I will see what I can do for you." Herr Stutze fills up his office. Full of energy, he sits down and I explain my position. He listens and agrees to help me. The good news is that in Switzerland the first meeting with a lawyer is free, the bad news is the costs that will come later. I wonder how Swiss men learn to protect their money so well. Do they learn it at school or in the playground? Is it in the air? Is it genetically imprinted? I imagine since the country was founded on the Swiss not paying their taxes to the Habsburgs it's in their collective unconscious. I see millions of Swiss men touching into their collective unconscious and farming a wealth of historical knowledge of how to pay just the right amount of taxes and alimony to ex-wives. The Swiss world I know is filled with hair-raising stories of lost battles in court over divorce settlements that first wives of very wealthy men should have gotten but didn't. It really takes a smart woman to outguess them. Someone's told me a Swiss woman has written a book called 'Don't marry Swiss men'. It's been censored in Switzerland. Not for the racy bits, don't worry about that, it's only because she gives some tips on how to get a decent settlement and beat the men at their own game. Censored! Can you imagine! But it shows you a country's priorities. In the middle of our discussions, I finally pluck up my courage and ask him what flag is swallowing us up, as it seems to be increasing its size on the wall behind him. Oh, it's just a Polynesian island, and I am one of their representatives. They live very differently from us, you know. They are an island people, very isolated.

"Have you seen magic performed at their ceremonies?" I ask.

"Yes of course," and with this he wips out of his suit jacket a small amulet. "I take it everywhere I go. You see, I am a very lucky man." My ears perk up.

"You know, I am writing a book about luck. Tell me more."

"Oh," he replies, "I usually get what I want. You see I am very focused. I see things very clearly."

"Well, that sounds like prepared luck," I answer. "You work hard, are terribly well informed about your subject and chances are that if you put your full energy flow behind it, it will work."

"You know," he continues, all terribly enthused about the subject.

Funny how talking about luck excites peoples' interest, perhaps they think if they talk about it they will find a way to become luckier.

"Well," he continues, "I was talking to a psychic who happens also to be a psychologist."

Boy, talking about covering all bases,

"and she said I was very lucky. She saw the field around me and she told me that my field attracts other lucky things to me."

Well, I mused, I need all the luck I can get, like Napoleon going into battle. I didn't need a good lawyer; I needed a lucky lawyer, *Luck, Luck, and Luck, Attorneys at Law.*

It is my second meeting with Herr Stutze. The in-between meeting being at a storage firm on the outskirts of Zürich where, after climbing over and opening twenty boxes, I finally found my divorce papers. Don't ever throw your divorce papers away or misplace them, you don't know it but your divorce lawyer may become a person you will talk to through the rest of your adult years. Also buried in this paper might be an overlooked fact that can change everything later. Well, Mr. Star Lawyer had arrived with quivering assistant and saw enough information to satisfy him to continue with our case. Back in his office, while discussing my case, I discovered that he was a very interesting man, a soldier in his youth, and now a lawyer, businessman, and aristocrat off to the family chateau immediately after our discussion. Suddenly, I jumped up, breaking up the meeting, and in a frantic voice told him that I must run downstairs and put two francs into a parking meter or get a fine of twenty.

"Yes, yes I understand you must do that." So, in between our discussion over my hoped-for millions and his multi-million deutschmark deals I am running into the streets for two francs. Honestly, every franc counts! It's the same when I go to my private bank. I walk through miles of marble hallways, am seated in a very grand private conference room, my distinguished banker tells me that, in order to save two francs a month in charges, he advises me to have my end-of-the-month statement sent to my other investment banker who will send it on to me. An interesting man. This lawyer, a man of different hats. He is a tactician who will be a worthy poker player against my ex. I will wait for his evaluation and I have given him the right to go ahead. As I leave he asks me if he can take me to dinner some time. Do lawyers usually do that? He is single. There must be a girlfriend in the background. He's attractive, but no, I think, not another Swiss man. But what, if he's lucky?

27.

A Word from Shakespeare

'There is a tide in the Affairs of men, which taken at the floods, leads on to fortune'

Shakespeare was one of the greatest writers of all time. As far as I'm concerned, he was also one of the world's greatest philosophers. I am sure that somewhere in his early life he had an epiphany. For one blinding moment in time, the world was illuminated to him in all its drama, abundance and diversity and like all great creative thinkers he just spent the rest of his life writing it all down. He saw that we are in flows of energy locked together in greater and greater circles of ever moving rivers of time. If once in someone's life this flow of swirling tide comes in to meet our timeless time and in that moment a creative act is formed with its new breath of energy, one must seize that moment. The same is true for a country or a person. For this flood of newly created energy will lead on, as he says, to fortune. Or to go one step, a quote from Robinson Jeffers:

> *The tides are in our veins, we still mirror*
> *the stars, life is your child but there is in*
> *me older and harder than life and more*
> *impartial the eye that watched before there was an Ocean'.*

We really are children of the stars. Most of the atoms in our hands were burning in the depth of some distant star. We really are, from the beginning, children of the Universe. We needed the death of stars to happen and compress the elements that we need for our bodies, carbon, nitrogen, and phosphorus. Our DNA has come down in us in an unbroken sequence from millions of years ago, all from a single micro-organism within which the universal genetic code first took its definitive form. Life, in that sense, is immortal.

Luck is an equal

opportunity employer.

Rich or poor can profit.

28.

A Word on Happiness

The American stock market plunged yesterday. It was one of the worst sell-offs in years. Everyone was running for cover. Dumping stocks like mad. God, doesn't anyone have courage any more? Has it always been like this or is it that they can not take this incredible run of luck the stock market has been having for years.

It's hard to separate Good from Lucky.

Frothy financial markets and a spate of take-overs on both sides of the Atlantic are yielding great returns for many money managers. Does that mean they're good investors? Not necessarily. "The challenge today is to distinguish the good managers from the lucky ones," said a wise consulant on Wall Street.

Well, I've got news for the grown-ups, look at what your children are buying. They are more plugged in than us and your money managers. Also, we just might run out of water and oil, so I'm stocking up on commodities.

Anyway, seated next to me in my favourite London coffee shop is a young journalist. He writes for G.Q., a magazine for men. I tell him about my book. He responds well. "Luck is when you feel that gut feeling in your stomach and you take the chance. The people who don't take that chance out of fear will never be lucky. The one that has the courage to take his chances, he's lucky. Life is making your own luck." He turns to me, "luckily your story is not about happiness, now that's a whole other story." He's right. The answer to what happiness is was explained in yesterday's International Herald Tribune. Happiness, defined as a sense of well-being according to many psychologists, is largely determined not by outside reality, but by our genetic make-up. Behavioral geneticists believe that we all have our genetic set points of happiness. Which means, whatever new job, new love affair, or exciting trip you take and get that buzz from, that new high will dissipate after six months and you'll once again return to your particular set point or level of happiness. How much is genetic and how much is the influences around you are still not decided. So, the good news is that the happy go lucky person you know today will be happy go lucky ten years from now. And you, out there neurotic, whining, complaining, given to moods and rarely happy will just have to sprinkle around you as many nice experiences as you can—a good meal, gardening, seeing favourite friends, working on a project you like. This will push your happiness level above your set point. The bad news is that if you're a sour personality, you'll remain one forever unless, like many Americans, you take a mood altering drug like Prozac which keeps you happy while you're taking it. So what's wrong with that?

Fate is our Destiny,

Luck comes and goes

29

Luck the American Way

Here's your American instant 30-day money back guaranteed politically correct program to become Lucky:
- You have gone through the bad luck in your last life, so this time around you are born under a lucky star. Lucky you, nothing to do. Enjoy. Proceed to Park place.
- You've still got some bad Karma left over, your present destiny doesn't look too promising. So, you've got to find out what kind of a time period you're in. This is crucial. There are certain times when you will have a luckier period than others. Time is not merely the measure of our days. So, how do you find what type of time you're in? Well, ...
- Two systems have been set up to understand the quality or character of our time frame. The I Ching is the most sophisticated divination method used for such purposes (you'll have to go into the Chinese community to find someone who practises this divination and if this person is not available search out a very good Astrologer). The Western Astrology chart is our attempt to read the meaning and character of man in terms of this quality of time. Those stars and planets are used only as mirrors to reflect our inner psychological patterns. There are moments in time when you are in a good period and life is more

conducive to good things happening. You can then actually take full advantage of it. Perhaps it's your early years that will go well for you, or your middle years, find out! It is really not worth huffing and puffing if you are in a bad time slot!!

There is also a time reading for a year. A Jon Sandiger in England practises this method. It is called "Nine House Astrology," "Nine Star Astrology" or "Nine Star Ki". It originated in Tibet, was practised in China and is now used extensively in Japan for astrological purposes. The system is based on the trigrams and hexagrams of the I Ching. These early interpretations have been refined by the Japanese and can be used very effectively in decision-making. It can answer: (one) Who you are? (two) Where you are in time? (three) The direction you are moving.

The system is mathematically based on nine-year cycles and has room to describe 108 different types of personalities. It is founded on nature; we are all represented by a part of nature. You have the choice to be water, soil, tree, metal or fire.

• Listen to the advice from a successful American businessman, Joseph Jaworski who has recently written a book *Synchronicity: The Inner Path of Leadership*, based on Jung's theory of synchronicity. Mr Jaworski applied its principles to his personal and business life. Through Mr Jaworski's search for meaning in his life and in the business world he discusses his conclusions on what these "predictable miracles or luck" are.

His feeling is that there is a deeper thought to life and that it is necessary to give up our ego, surrender to knowing that whatever we need at the moment to meet our destiny will be available to us. Not easy for us to do, just stand and be. He narrows the time frame down for us and suggests that we must wait expectantly with acute awareness for that cubic centimetre of chance to present itself. And when it does, he says, we must act with lightning speed and almost without conscious reasoning to take 'the chance'. It is at this point that our freedom and destiny merge and we create the future into which we are living. A certain flow of meaning begins and when you are in this state of surrender you exert an enormous attractiveness because of your authentic presence. He explains in his book that the way we've been taught to outwit the next person, stick with it no matter what, seize fate by the throat, and do whatever it takes to succeed in the end is limited and emotionally unsatisfactory.

His thoughts to start this flow and tap into this streak of predictable miracles is to:

- Change the mental model of the world from causal "A + B = C thinking" to an open dynamic all interconnected open universe.

- Realize that all events and people are related. There is a relationship to all.

- The nature of our commitment must change from doing whatever it takes to succeed to putting oneself into a state of surrender to our destiny. He did it, it worked, and what he learned was implemented at the highest levels of American business to great success.

- Now here's the problem: you've got the right time and the right attitude, but do you know what you want? Contrary to a million self-help realization books it's hard to know yourself, for reasons quite complicated that I'm not going to get into right now, let alone know what you really want. However, I think, in great emotional moments you can come close to knowing the real you. Next time you're mad or cry over something, or have a lump in your throat or really get mad—stop a moment and study why you have been moved so much. These are clues to what matters to you. Mull over your memories and dreams, your wishes will be tied into them, learn to meditate and listen to music. Music sets your thoughts free to daydream and think. It touches a deeper level we don't normally have access to; it taps into our unconscious. I've always felt guilty at concerts when my mind has wandered away from a beautiful symphony, but this is part of the Yin-Yang flow of music. Music gives us another experience of life. It is real and truly touches who we are. It is a key to open the door to who you are and what you want out of life. There's an old Rock and Roll song that has the truth of the centuries in it. It starts "Life is but a dream, it's what you make it." So wake up and follow your dreams.

- Listen to the Chinese. They say, "good fortune and misfortune take effect through perseverance". The secret of action lies in duration. Good fortune and misfortune are slow in the making. Only when a trend is followed continuously do the results of single actions gradually accumulate in such a way that they manifest as good fortune or misfortune.

- New findings in Dr Richard Wiseman's research into 'lucky' people at the University of Hertfordshire shows that "the people judged to be lucky do things differently from the rest of us, including putting their trust in their intuitions and going with hunches." So next time, trust your intuition!

30.

A Word about the Chinese
Ancient Chinese

All civilizations have attempted to divine the future and to understand their reality. Our Ancients would use the simplest form of divination, throw some chicken bones on the floor, twigs, pebbles, and read the answer, Yes or No. Hit or miss. It is still used today. What was different with the Chinese was that they realized intuitively that there were other energies at play in this simple act. They realized the importance of mathematics as a tool to understand this process and therefore brought the whole process of divination unto a much higher level of sophistication. In their world, a mathematician was also an astronomer and an astrologer and this knowledge up until recently was only used for the purpose of divination. Now, before we dive into the two powerful tools that were developed by them to increase one's luck in life, the I Ching and Feng Shui, I'd like to explain some of the philosophical background of the Chinese for it is very different from ours and one that we can learn a great deal from.

Chinese philosophy is based on humanism or, in other words, the human being and his relationship to the physical world. There is just humankind, sandwiched between Heaven and Earth. Their philosophy has played the role for them that our Judeo-Christian religion has played for us. And the central question that their philosophy deals with was how could man improve himself and aspire to greatness on this earth? To be a gentleman of learning and distinction was the aim. They believed that Heaven, the stars and the constellations of the stars influenced the situations on earth. It was summed up in the radical Shih, the divine influence by which the Will of Heaven, or Tao governed earthly things. This radical Shih was to manifest so to speak the hidden will of the divinity of Tao and that was also at the same time the radical for calculation. The Ancients did not look for yes or no, but how a situation fitted into their great world of Yin and Yang, the two polar forces which govern the Universe. The Yin representing the passive female principle and the Yang the active male. The two constantly interacting to create all things and all developments. When the Yin situation prevailed one must act in a Yin manner, in a Yang time more aggressive and bold. Having the wise attitude that nothing is absolutely good or absolutely bad one has to act in the proper manner to the time. Western thought is more egocentric. It asks is it good or bad for me. The Chinese were detached and philosophical enough to say that even if it's bad for me it might be good for the whole. From the beginning they had a wise and more objective view of what we call good and bad and saw it more as something in the ensemble of existence. In a way it was the beginning of science. It had the essentials of what we call the experimental method. For there is a question in the mind of the one who asks and a mathematical method for approaching the chaos of existence and then drawing a conclusion. That is what is done in most modern physical experiments. Western man wants to know what the situation will lead to. The Chinese are the other way around. They live in the idea of the wholeness so they can act in the awareness of it.

This philosophy is derived from their ancient cosmology and came out of the many competing schools called the Hundred. Over time the ideas were incorporated into the I Ching which described the cosmological principles of the Universe and elaborated them in ways that could be divined through patterns of hexagrams and the meanings attached to them. This Book of Changes, or I Ching, was one of their six classics that corresponded to our Western liberal arts. They included The Book of History, Music, Book of Odes, Rituals or Rites, and Spring and Autumn Annals. For them, the Universe had an ultimate basic numerical rhythm, conceived as a number pattern. All relationships of things with each other in all areas of outer and inner life mirror this same basic number pattern in a form conceived as a rhythm. Everything is outwardly and inwardly in a flux of energy that follows certain basic and recurring numerical rhythms. In all areas of events one would always finally arrive at this mirror image, the basic rhythm-a-matrix of the cosmos.

Field of Time

The Chinese believed that we live in two time orders, the eternal and the heavenly. The underlying numerical order of eternity is Ho Tou, the eternal order of the timeless time where the Universe; Heaven and Earth are opposite each other with the elements arranged accordingly. All the archetypal possibilities are arranged on an archetypal field. The elements are in energic connection, but do not fight each other. They do not move, it's more like a dragonfly hovering in midair. It moves, but remains stationary full of tensions and inner vibration. It is the world of our unconscious. This unconscious psyche cannot predict synchronistic and other events very accurately, but by using the I Ching it will refer to the quality of a time, a moment where a synchronistic event might occur. It is a key moment, a certain moment in time which is the uniting factor but it is a blurred image of possibilities. This synchronistic thinking takes in the physical and psychic at that moment and answers the question: What likes to happen together?

The other part of the time order, which came later, the heavenly order or Lo Shou, is the one we live in. It is a magic square that sets the basic rhythm. It is built up mathematically and moves in a human time cycle. The Chinese discovered this matrix intuitively and for them it represented a basic mirror or rhythmic image of the universe seen in a time aspect. We live normally with our consciousness in cyclic time, it is the world of our A plus B equals C thinking, but there is the other eternal time, the Ho Tou underneath which sometimes interferes with the other. That's where luck or chance comes in when these two meet. So, it is essential to watch both areas of reality, the physical and the psychic, all is connected.

The Ho Tou
Timeless Time

7

2

8 3 5 4 9

1

6

Lo Shu — Fen Shui
Later Heavenly Order

The Lo Shu is one of the basic matrices or arrangements of the Universe in a quadrangular matrix, a magic square. It is magic because whichever way you add up the figures the result is always fifteen and it is the only square which has only three elements in each row or column.

4	9	2
3	5	7
8	1	6

The Chinese watched both areas of reality, the physical and the psychic, and noticed that at a certain moment when one had these and these thoughts or these and these dreams which would be the psychological events, such and such outer physical events had to happen. There was a complex of physical and psychological events in a certain key moment of time that was the uniting factor, the focal point, for the observation of this complex of events. It could be a cluster of events or it could be one event. The future is always present as a seed. If we know the kernel point of a situation we can predict its consequences. And if we know the deepest underlying archetypal constellation of our present situation then we can, to a certain extent, know how things will go. The future is present in the unconscious but it may take a lifetime to realize.

Now, these two incompatible systems have to come together and the only place where they link up is in the center where there is no doubleness. They link in a nowhere, or in a hole. So in this hole in time, in measured time, man steps in and something happens. It is a truly creative time. Something new is created. It is Mr. Jaworski's cubic centimeter of chance. Where his or anyone's luck happens!

31

The I Ching or Book of Changes / Feng Shui

'In ancient times the holy sages made the Book of Changes. Thus, they invented the Yarrow stalk oracle in order to lend aid in a mysterious way to the light of the gods.

To heaven they assigned the number three and to Earth the number two. From these they computed the other numbers. They contemplated the changes in the dark and the light and established the hexagrams in accordance with them. They brought about movements in and the yielding, and thus produced the individual lines.

They put themselves in accord with tao (natural law) and its power, and in conformity with this laid down the order of what is right. By thinking through the order of the outer world to the end and by exploring the law of their nature to the deepest core, they arrived at an understanding of fate.'

(Taken from The Eight Winds, Sho Kua, Discussion of
the Trigrams, containing material of great antiquity in
explanation of the eight primary trigrams.)

The Book of Changes or I Ching, one of the most important books in world literature comes to us through the mists of antiquity. Developed from a collection of lines comprised of eight trigrams, it has influenced all of Chinese Cultural life since 5000 B.C. when it is said that the great Chinese sage Fu-Hsi intuitively thought out the order of Heaven and Earth and everything that was part of it. He thought out the order of the external world down to its ultimate constituents and the law of their own inwardness down to its deepest core. He encompassed just everything and in this way succeeded in understanding fate. He devised the eight trigrams, a triagram being three lines stacked up on each other called the Sequence of Earlier Heaven, these were later expanded to six lines stacked up. These lines are either broken (-—-) or completed (＿＿) and consist of sixty-four hexagrams in all. These hexagrams represent every conceivable condition between Heaven and Earth. They follow the laws of eternal changes; they are images that are constantly undergoing changes. Each one represents one of the elements, a certain process of nature and a specific member of a family consisting of a father, mother, three sons and three daughters (they actually represent functions, a daughter represents devotion, for example).

Li The Clinging, Fire
Li means to cling to something

——————————————————

———————— ————————

——————————————————

——————————————————

———————— ————————

——————————————————

The <u>image</u> is fire
The <u>judgement</u> based on the Clinging is perseverance

(The proper interpretation of this hexagram takes up five pages in the I Ching.)

All 64 hexagrams are paired with a number and the individual lines. Where the lines in the hexagram fall and their corresponding number is very important.

Now, up until 1150 B.C. these hexagrams were mute. It was left to King Wen and his son the Duke of Chow to give meaning or Judgements to these hexagrams. They arranged them into their present form. A world formula of natural philosophy for the individual was found. The Changes of Chow subsequently took on more of a divination text. His judgements clothed the images with words, indicating whether an action will bring good fortune, misfortune, remorse or humiliation. These judgements make it possible to decide what type of action is necessary, whether one should resist a course of action or proceed. For it is only at the very beginning of a situation that the Chinese believe you can change your fate. Once the momentum starts it's too late to change.

To divine what these hexagrams meant fifty Yarrow stalks were used. The ancients believed it was a sacred plant representing the Vegetable Kingdom, the other two kingdoms being man and animals, all three pulsated to different rhythms. Using the Yarrow stalks connected their vibrations. Chance came to be utilized as the fourth medium. For the very absence of an immediate meaning in chance left space for a deeper meaning to come through.

Not everyone could use this oracle. Men must approach these humble divining stalks with clear and tranquil minds, receptive to the cosmic influences hidden in the stalks. Holding in their minds an intuitive mental model of the spirit of the times they would manipulate these yarrow stalks dividing and redividing them eighteen times. Then, using their mathematical system of whole numbers, they would arrive at a number between one and sixty-four, open the book, turn to the appropriate hexagram and, in the spirit of that moment, interpret that particular hexagram.

You can try it yourself if you can find some Yarrow stalks (coins are used but are not as good). But having a dialogue with an ancient book is quite an extraordinary experience. I can only reckon that this ancient book works as a sort of network of electric circuits, which penetrates everything. By asking a question you switch on the current and then a certain part of the network is lit up. But it doesn't light up unless the person asking the question has somehow in himself or herself established contact with a definite situation.

Funny that my quest ends with the I Ching, 'A world order Formula' thought up before recorded time. But, even more astonishing is a book I recently read called the I Ching and the Genetic Code. In it, the author shows the link between science and spirituality with the discovery that the 64 triplets of the DNA discovered in our century matches up with the 64 hexagrams of the I Ching in a revolutionary way. Watson and Crick's life code meets an ancient philosophical world order. The results of his work make fascinating reading.

Feng Shui

The Chinese have always been a civilization interested in increasing their luck. They believe there is a trinity of forces that make up ones luck in life. Heaven Luck (our fate)—what we are born with, whether we will be rich or poor, destined for greatness or great tragedy. This cannot be changed and is explained through Chinese Astrology. Then comes, Man Luck, that which is created by our own actions. This is where our hard work and perseverance comes in. To help us along the different paths of life the I Ching is meant to guide us. This great book of wisdom helps us decide what directions to take to attain our fullest human potential. And then last, but not least, the third force, Earth Luck. This comes from our environment. Feng Shui, considered part of the philosophy of the I Ching, is the tool they have developed to bring together the external forces of nature with the internal environment to create a balanced and peaceful dwelling in order to create a luckier environment.

Feng Shui offers guidelines and specific measures for activating all the different aspects of luck in one's life. It is concerned with harnessing the earth's Chi, or life force of the universe. Balancing these three types of luck in a harmonious balance will bring enormous good fortune into one's life. Since Feng Shui properly applied can bring luck in all areas of life: health, wealth, power, fame, and martial bliss to name a few, I decided to call up a Feng Shui master. As I was told, if you don't know what you are doing you can make it worse. I called in Thomas Wang, a practising master trained in the art of placement to see what I could do to push that Earth Luck along. After a serious walkabout in my home, consulting his compass, the news was not too bad. I could not eat anything cooked on my oven. It was wrongly placed, the gas was coming out in the wrong direction. This didn't particularly disturb me since I rarely use it. People tend to eat out a lot in London, as I consider my refrigerator, a Holly Golightly refrigerator, holding at most times two bottles of Champagnes. The bed in my bedroom was positioned completely wrong and actually, where I should be sleeping is in my son's room. 'Thomas, I am not going to give up my beautiful big bedroom to sleep in that tiny bedroom', I cried. Two inscrutably piercing oriental eyes pinned me down. 'That is your best corner and that is where you should be writing and sleeping.' Well, I did what he said. My son took the news that he would be forced to sleep in my enormously comfortable bedroom for his Easter holiday rather well. He was nice enough to comment on what a good mattress I had.

The Chinese believe that in every woman's lifetime she has several chances for marriage. Some opportunities are better than others. If she arranges her home in a way to promote her luck she will improve her chances for happiness in a good relationship. So, the good corners of my rooms were activated, plants were put in the proper position and, after some pushing and pulling of furniture, I was ready.

Feng Shui doesn't come cheap. So, while you're saving up your money to hire someone who knows what he is doing, I can give you some general hints on what one shouldn't do. Don't have mirrors in your bedroom, especially if they face your bed. Buy a book on Feng Shui; ask your local bookstore which one they recommend. It should explain the principles of Feng Shui to start you on your way. Once you've figured out which are your lucky corners you can start to activate them with flowers, crystals, plants. Hopefully, your toilet, kitchen and storerooms are properly placed. Otherwise they can wash away your luck. And if the door to your house is not facing the right direction you're really in big trouble. Don't laugh about this. There is not a serious company, Western or Asian, that does not consult these Feng Shui masters before they construct those high-rise buildings that are sprouting up all over Asia.

32

Modern Chinese Thoughts

Now that I've thoroughly convinced you that the Ancient Chinese have the answer and you've run out to find a local Chinese fortune-teller and eaten lots of Chinese food in preparation, I thought I'd better check with a modern Chinese person to see what today's Chinese think.

Modern thoughts on luck were told to me by a young Chinese Buddhist Orthodontist seated among piles of second-hand clothes being sorted out by lots of Chinese women getting ready for a fair to be held the following week.

Young man:" Please sit down. I will try to do my best to give you our idea of what luck is.

You know, our philosophy has over the years combined Confucius, Tao, and Buddhism, so we have our unique religion as opposed to Thailand, India, etc. For us, luck has to do with Karma. What your past life was like, how many good deeds you did, accumulates in energy and is given in the form of talent, health, or luck (smooth sailing through life). It's like having a current account. If you overdraw you become a deficit. If you give deeply your good deeds build up your credit. It is a cause and effect on the karmic cycle. For animals, nature and people are all on this cycle. The cycle has a spirit. The lowest being ghosts, the very highest Buddha. We can, through our own efforts, become a Buddha and break our karmic cycle. We all have the past, present and future in us and there are monks who have evolved and developed their supernatural abilities to the point that they can see through to other peoples past lives. One has to clear one's mind. Have eyes of crystal. The Chinese discourage fortune telling for they believe that if you know certain events it will happen, you will act differently. But it is very prevalent in our lives."

"Thank you very much," I say as I rise to leave.

"Remember," he says, smiling, "Red is for us a very lucky color."

33.

The Quality of Time

The quality of time I moved in was quixotic, unsure, the floor was somehow taken out from under us. Time moved faster, stock markets worldwide soared beyond comprehension— and then plummeted. Unemployment was on the other hand reaching unsustainable levels; France and Germany were at their breaking points. Humankind continued its vicious, religious and ethnic wars, faceless terrorists roamed the world causing havac in their wake, huge stresses were pulling the world in all directions. There were no superpowers anymore to hit the little guys on the head. Russia had no more money and America was turning inwards, limiting themselves to their own worries. Science was throwing new discoveries at us a mile a minute, genetically modified foods, the whole human genome mapped out opening the way to a much healthier longer-living society. The moral choices overwhelmed us. Entertainment distractions bombarded us. Movies, computers, theater, 140 channels on television, mobile phones, music, sports, motion, ... and in all this I tried to be ... just be.

Notable Persons' Thoughts on Luck

Everything in life, I believe, is luck and timing."

Pamela Harriman
(American Ambassador to France)

Work hard. Share. Be lucky."

Michael Blomberg
(Visionary leader of the world's fastest growing media empire)

Talking of his relationship with Soon-Yi that it is *"good luck, just good luck ... that is what is so interesting about relationships."*

Woody Allen
(American actor, writer)

34.

Moment in Time

And what of Marie-Louise and Karl? Well, Marie-Louise's mother died just at that point Mr Right entered. Someone she had known over the years. He flew in to pay his respects and whisked her off to Brazil. So rich and handsome. Creepy, Marie-Louise told me later, her mother had met her husband at her sister's funeral. Anyway, her moment had come and she grabbed it. And Karl, well, he is waiting to start his prison term. Knowing him, he's probably looking forward to it. Figuring his term will not be too long—a few years and then he'll be out and about. Karl, always im Gluck.

But, I can learn something from Karl. And that is, if one looks at things in a more optimistic slant events seem to appear more lucky then they are and before you know it you begin to think you're luckier than you are. I recalled that fateful day when I awoke with the realization that I was not lucky, but after having a good talk to myself, I realized I was much luckier than I thought. I had no terrible diseases, I had a loving family, my life was relatively stress-free, and there was almost enough money in the bank and I didn't have to live with someone I wasn't happy with.

So, I got my Feng Shui in order and waited. Now, you're not going to believe this, but once that was done, two days later a friend of mine told me a production company was interested in my children's book for a series. A letter arrived in the post from this publisher saying they were interested in this story and someone whom I hadn't heard from in a long time came rushing back into my life. The tide was moving in my direction ...

So, I leave you in my moment of time and wish you 'Lots of Luck'.

Bibliography

The following books have proved an invaluable source of reference:

Broad CD, Philosophy, volume XXIV, 1949, pages 291-309.

Csikszentmihalyi M, Flow, Rider, 1972.

von Franz M-L, On Divination and Synchronicity, Inner City Books, Toronto, Canada.

Dobbs A, cited in Koestler A, "Janus", Hutchinson of London, 1978, page 271.

Gwathmey E, Lots of Luck, Angel City Press. 1994.

Jaworski J, Synchronicity, Berrett-Koehler Publishers, 1996.

Jung CG, Synchronicity: An Acausal Conncecting Principle in Jung-Pauli, Eine Naturerklärung und Psyche, Studium aus dem CG Jung-Institut in Zürich, 1952.

Koestler A, Janus, Hutchinson of London, 1978.

Koestler A., The Roots of Coincidence, Hutchinson of London, 1972.

Lawrence R, Unlock your Psychic Powers, Souvenir Press, 1993, pages 184-187.

Price HH, cited in Koestler A, Janus, Hutchinson of London, 1978, page 271.

van der Post L, Jung and the Story of our Time, Vitage Books, 1975.

Schönberger M, The I Ching and the Genetic Code, Aurora Press, 1992.

Wilhelm R, The I Ching (translation), Bollinger Foundation 1950.